MW01487287

WITCH DANCE

Lori Crane

To Elizabeth with love,

Lori Crane

Lori Crane

Copyright 2018 Lori Crane Entertainment
All rights reserved, including the right to reproduce this book or any
portion thereof in any form whatsoever.
For information, please email LoriCraneAuthor@gmail.com.

Published by Lori Crane Entertainment
Edited by Elyse Dinh-McCrillis at TheEditNinja.com
Cover design: Rob Hess

This book is a work of historical fiction.
Some names, characters, places, and incidents are from historical
accounts.
Some names, characters, places, and incidents are products of the
author's imagination.

ISBN: 978-0-9964295-3-5
eBook ISBN: 978-0-9964295-4-2

Praise for Lori Crane

"Lori Crane's writing is magnetic...she pulls you in with her unabashed honesty, eloquent simplicity, historical genealogical knowledge and pastoral care of each and every character."
 ~Amazon customer for *Okatibbee Creek*

"Lori Crane is a Southern storyteller of the first order."
~*Writer's Digest* for *The Legend of Stuckey's Bridge*

"This is a five-star book written by a five-star author."
~ Readers' Favorite for *An Orphan's Heart*

 "Crane writes with great attention to detail and an authentic historical feel."
~ Christoph Fischer, award-winning author of *The Luck of the Weissensteiners* and *Sebastian*

"As always, Ms. Crane delivers a great story. Descriptions are precise, the dialogue flows easily, and the characters are well rounded."
~ Anna Belfrage, award-winning author of *The Graham Saga*

"This is a five-star winner and Lori Crane is a must-read author."
~ Readers' Favorite for *The Legend of Stuckey's Bridge*

 "I was hooked from the first page to the last."
~Amazon customer for *I, John Culpepper*

"Elly Hays by Lori Crane is a rare gem... A historically rich tale where there are really no bad guys...a page-turning read."
~Readers' Favorite for *Elly Hays*

"If you like Southern legend and folklore, this series is for you."
~Amazon customer for *The Stuckey's Bridge Trilogy*

Table of Contents

Witch Dance Trailhead Sign

Milepost 233.2

Natchez Trace Parkway, Mississippi

"Witch Dance
The very name conjures visions of eerie
midnights,
swirling black capes, and brooms
stacked against a nearby tree!
The old folks say the witches once
gathered here to dance,
and that wherever their feet touched the
ground,
the grass withered and died, never to
grow again.
Impossible?
Maybe so, but look around.
Look for a hidden spot where no grass
grows."

United States Department of the Interior
National Park Service

Bynum Mounds

Milepost 232.4

Natchez Trace Parkway, Mississippi

Thousands of years before the first Europeans set foot on what is now the United States of America, indigenous peoples made their home on the continent. Descendants of the Toltecs of Mexico, the Hopewell Indians, migrated to the area now known as Tupelo, Mississippi around 100 BC. Their leaders were brothers Chiksa and Chata. Legend has it the brothers had a disagreement so terrible it split the tribe in two. The two factions became the modern-day Chickasaws and Choctaws.

Around 100 BC, this Hopewell tribe created the Bynum Mounds. There are six mounds in all, ranging from five to fourteen feet in height.

In the 1940s, the mounds were excavated by the National Park Service and found to be burial sites for these indigenous people. The NPS identified the cremated remains of a woman with copper bracelets on her wrists, the traces of two additional adults, and the remnants of a child.

Also excavated from the site were artifacts of greenstone axe heads, copper spools, and shiny pieces of galena. Greenstone, copper, and galena do not originate in Mississippi.

Chapter 1

August 25, 2018

Emily and Sarah squealed as they raced toward the small hills at the edge of the field. No tree or bush grew on top of the hills. They were two barren knolls of smooth earth, offering neatly manicured grass and clear views of the surrounding land. Except for the Bynum Mounds tourist sign at the parking lot entrance, no one would even know what these mounds were. The six-year-old girls knew nothing of the history of these hills. They were only concerned with beating each other to the top.

They ran as fast as their legs could run. This was nothing new; they raced everywhere. They'd done so since before they learned to walk, crawling faster and faster to beat the other to the prize at the end of the race. Born mere minutes apart, they displayed typical sibling rivalry while vying for a favorite toy or the brightest crayon. Their favorite competition was racing each other.

Margaret and Thomas Speedwell had driven down the Natchez Trace from Nashville for a long overdue getaway with their girls. They'd arrived the day before, excited for their weekend camping trip at a place just north of the Bynum Mounds, a campground called Witch Dance.

Witch Dance sounded like a fun place to spend the weekend. It sported its own elaborate history, rumored to be where witches held their rituals and ceremonies. Legend has it that witches danced around bonfires, and where their feet touched the ground, no grass ever grew again, even until this day. The sign stating the legend at the entrance of the campground was a popular spot for photos by people who visited the site—families, ghost hunters, and the curious. The Speedwell family didn't come for ghost hunting. This weekend was simply a chance for Margaret, Thomas, and their girls to shed the stress of their everyday lives and have a little fun.

"I wish they wouldn't run ahead like that," Margaret grumbled from the parking lot.

"It's okay. Let them run," Thomas replied. "We can see them from here."

Thomas saw Margaret's forehead crease with concern. She had a strand of black hair lying across her ivory cheek, but he resisted the temptation to brush it off her face. She was wound up, and if he touched her when she wasn't expecting it, she would jump, then apologize for being so jittery, then become even more anxious. Instead, he reached for her hand, touching her fingers first, then moving his palm into hers. She allowed him to hold her hand as they strolled toward the mounds, following their daughters. The lack of shrubbery and trees made it easy to keep an eye on the girls, but Thomas knew that still wouldn't help Margaret relax.

"But they always run," she said. "They run through the grocery store, the playground, the parking lot. I've scolded them a million times but I can't get them to stop racing, no matter the punishment. What if they fall? What if they get hurt?"

Thomas squeezed her hand. "Oh, let them go.

They won't get hurt. You worry too much, Mama Hen." He chuckled softly, attempting to lighten her mood.

Margaret pouted.

Thomas knew his feeble attempt at humor wasn't going to make his wife's concerns disappear. She was overly cautious when it came to the girls—paranoid, even. She fretted over every movement, every vegetable at every meal, the length of every nap. She hadn't always been this obsessive, but with each miscarriage, each still birth, Margaret had grown more and more cautious. When they were finally blessed with the girls, Margaret's caution became even more irrational. If Thomas brought up that fact, it would be the beginning of the next round of arguments, and end with her crying and accusing him of not loving her anymore, at which point he would disappear into his study or leave the house and bury himself in work at his office.

She yanked her hand away from his when they heard Emily shriek, the blood draining from Margaret's already pale face. Even Thomas's adrenaline shot straight up at the sound, and he jerked his head in the direction of the girls. He and Margaret both caught their breath when they saw the girls laughing, Sarah chasing Emily to the top of one of the hills.

***

Emily shrieked as Sarah grabbed the back of her pink shirt, attempting to catch up, but the material slipped from Sarah's fingers. Emily reached her hand back for Sarah, and they giggled as Emily pulled her sister forward. Their blond curls, which they inherited from their father, bounce as they crossed over the ridge at the top. They had begun their descent down the other side when they stopped in their tracks, their eyes wide.

On this hot summer day with a crystal blue sky and bright sunshine, a large cloud floated in front of them. Not a puffy white cloud—more like a murky shadow. It slowly swirled about a foot above the ground, as if an imaginary wind was trying to create a tornado, but there was no wind, not even the slightest breeze. The site resembled the twister the girls had seen in the movie with Dorothy and Toto, but there was no dirt or debris or houses in the vortex, just blackness.

The girls stood still, squeezing each other's hand. Emily wanted to scream for her mother, but she could only open and close her mouth like a fish washed up on a beach. It was as if the shadow had sucked all the air out of her lungs.

The black cloud began to increase in size, and the winds picked up. The howling winds started as a low hum and grew louder and louder until it became a frightening sound, simultaneously emitting an ear-piercing shriek and a low, agonizing moan.

The girls released each other's hands and covered their ears.

The whirlwind continued to grow, inching closer to them, pulling at their curls, their clothing.

Even with her hands over her ears, Emily thought she heard human voices mumbling something beneath the roar of wind. She squinted her eyes and cocked her head, as if doing so would make the voices clearer. She felt Sarah reach for her arm, but Emily couldn't take her eyes off the cloud. Sarah took a step forward, trying to pull Emily with her, but Emily stepped backward. Sarah's fingers again lost their grip.

Emily took a second step backward. Everything in her gut told her to turn and run in the opposite direction. Back to her mother, back to her father, back to safety. She sensed something bad in the shadow before them and was certain it was watching them and wishing them to come closer.

Sarah reached back again for Emily, but Emily took another step backward, staying just out of her sister's reach. Then Emily turned and ran back up the hill, faster than she had ever run before. She was certain Sarah would follow. Sarah always followed.

The moment she reached the top of the hill, the roaring stopped. The whirring, the voices, and the wind vanished. Emily saw her parents casually strolling toward the hill. Why weren't they running? Didn't they hear the horrible tornado that almost gobbled up their children?

Emily turned around to look for Sarah. There was nothing behind her but the bright, sunny valley below. No sound, no tornado, no Sarah.

Emily collapsed like a rag doll.

Chapter 2

The Eighth Full Moon, 100 BC

Chata and Chiksa stood in front of nearly a thousand people, many of whom had traveled great distances to pay their final respects to the great chief. Their wives, both great with child, stood beside them in the place of honor reserved for immediate family. At the foot of the hill, in front of the growing crowd, sat a large cypress box containing the chief's remains. Artisans had painstakingly hand-carved the coffin with intricate woodland animals, geometric designs, pine trees, and a blazing sun. It had taken many hours to create the masterpiece, a great work of art to honor a great man. Too bad it would be destroyed in the cremation that would follow the presentation of the gifts.

The Bynum chief had been admired and respected by his tribe and the surrounding tribes and had been a beloved father to his twins, Chata and Chiksa. He'd been a direct descendant of the mighty Hopewell Indian chief who had brought the tribe from Mexico to this land many decades earlier. The stories passed down through generations told of the tribe's harrowing escape from their homeland. For years, they had faced a collapsing government, which culminated in a war over depleted food sources. During the war, a group of Hopewell people fled their land and searched for many moons for a new place to call home, a nonviolent place to rebuild their shattered lives, a fertile place to feed their people, a safe place to raise their children. Many had starved and died along the way, but even with the great losses, the people traveled with hope for the future, grateful to leave the political oppression behind. It wasn't easy to leave their land and homes, and it was impossible to do so without the sacred bones of their beloved Toltec ancestors. Carrying the dried bones, they headed north, and after a lengthy and strenuous journey, they reached a land where they believed they could rebuild their lives.

Before they even built the first shelter, they honored their ancestors by burying the dried bones in sacred mounds and declaring the surrounding land a holy place. Those outside the Bynum tribe named the burial sites the Bynum Mounds, and all nearby tribespeople held them in great reverence. For decades, subsequent members of the tribe had also been buried there, and the mounds had grown larger with each passing generation. Today, they would bury their great chief in the sacred place.

The carved box holding his remains rested atop a large altar, and in front of it, an enormous pile of grave offerings was growing by the second. Citizens of the community, from the elders to the smallest children, were lined up to place their gifts before the altar. There were so many treasures, the altar itself was nearly no longer visible.

Molded silhouettes of jaguars, coyotes, and eagles were placed on the parched ground at the base of the altar. Finely polished stones, bear claw pendants, painted fabrics, seashells, figurines of women in robes and men in loincloths dotted the top of the pile. Hundreds of effigies of animals and humans were squeezed in wherever there was room, draped with bracelets, masks, and ear spools made from copper. Specially made bowls and cups, carved and painted, were piled a foot deep. Beaded garments lay next to bleached wolf jaws and dried rattlesnake skins. The coffin was laden with fruits, squash, and maize, as well as simple offerings of flowers and beans.

Chata and Chiksa stood motionless for hours observing the proceedings, proud that their father was so well loved by his people.

"Your father will be greatly missed," Salina whispered to her husband.

"Yes," replied Chiksa, "and by none more so than his grandchild." He reached over and rubbed her swollen belly.

Tears glistened on Salina's dark lashes and dripped onto her deerskin dress, causing dark spots to speckle the garment. "I'm sorry he won't be here to meet your child."

"I'm sorry, too, but we'll make sure the child is told all the stories of the great legend that was his grandfather."

Chiksa smiled at his wife, admiring her bronze skin and perfect braids, held in place by a feathered and beaded headdress she'd made especially for the occasion. She was the most beautiful woman in the entire clan, and would be regal as the clan's new chieftainess and mother of the next chief. This pregnancy, her first, certainly agreed with her. Her face glowed with health and vigor.

He glanced past her at his brother. "Chata, are you all right?"

Chata nodded but didn't say anything. He continued staring forward, watching the people paying their respects. His face was expressionless, his dark eyes dull, but there was a hint of pain around the down-turned corners of his mouth.

Chata had always been the quieter and more sensitive of the brothers, and hadn't said more than a few words since their father died two days ago. Chiksa knew his brother's moods. While Chata was usually quiet, he had never been this sullen. Chata wasn't all right, but Chiksa didn't know what he could do to help him.

Chiksa turned his attention back to the long line of people leaving gifts. He was honored to be here but had to admit he was growing physically tired of standing in the same spot. He shifted his weight to his other foot and tucked his long hair behind his ear as he glanced back at Chata. He wished Chata would say something, anything. They were now the leaders of the Bynum clan, and their people needed to know they would be safe, that their lives would not be disrupted following this great loss. Chiksa wished for a sign of reassurance from his brother, but what he saw was anything but encouraging.

***

A small boy wearing only a buckskin loincloth and moccasins walked up to the altar and placed a single flower on the pile of gifts. Chata watched as the boy, no more than seven or eight, faced the altar and stood stone-still, as if praying. Chata admired the silky black braid that hung halfway down the child's back; the boy reminded him of Chiksa at that age. The boy carried himself the same way, as if the world must take notice. When the child turned to leave, he paused and looked straight at Chata. The boy looked as if he wanted to say something or maybe run over and hug Chata. This boy Chata had never seen before seemed to know exactly how he was feeling. Yes, the boy reminded him of his brother. Chiksa had always read Chata with a single look, and Chata had seen this exact look from Chiksa on many occasions, especially in the last two days.

Chata glanced now at Chiksa, who didn't seem to notice the boy. He was staring straight ahead. His muscular arms were folded across his bare chest, an oxtail tied around his bicep. His jaw was firm. He looked like a mountain—immovable, impenetrable. The only softness to him was the feather that hung from his hair. It bounced gently with each puff of breeze. Chiksa was a strong man. He would become a great chief.

Chata wished he could be more like Chiksa. He wished he knew how to put on a brave face like Chiksa was doing. Chata was well aware his brother had been worried about him these last two days, and honestly, he was worried about himself. He had never felt so alone and sad. He didn't mean to place that burden on Chiksa, but Chiksa had always voluntarily carried the burdens. No one ever asked him to. He was just that kind of man.

Chiksa turned to Chata, with concern in his eyes. The warrior was only tough on the outside. Inside he was warm and caring.

Chata feigned a slight smile to try to convince Chiksa he was fine. He knew Chiksa was right, that Chata needed to emerge from this sadness and show his people he had the strength to lead them. He hadn't told Chiksa, but their father's death was not the only thing weighing on Chata's mind. He also worried about his wife, Mia.

Mia was hugely pregnant with twins, which frightened Chata. Her animal-hide dress couldn't hide the fact she was enormous and growing larger by the day. He didn't even know how his petite wife was still on her feet for this long in her condition. She had carried the twins thus far with no problem, but following the chief's death, Chata had begun thinking a lot about his mother, whom he'd never known. She had died giving birth to him and Chiksa. The thoughts of his mother's death set off a fear he couldn't control. His wife delivering twins at any time had him filled with dread. He prayed daily to the gods for Mia's protection and for the welfare of his unborn children.

He realized he wasn't breathing. He took in a deep breath, released it, and turned back to the proceedings. He looked at the coffin. His father was an extraordinary man. He had not only led the clan but raised two boys alone. He'd never taken another wife, never loved another woman except Chata and Chiksa's mother. Chata hoped she and his father had found each other again somewhere in the spirit realm. He wished for their happiness, but more than anything, at this very moment, he wished for the one thing he couldn't have: his father's guidance. He needed his father's strength, his father's wisdom. He needed to know how to be a good father, how to protect his wife, although he wasn't sure his father could teach him that latter skill when the chief hadn't been able to save his own wife.

Chata felt like the boy still standing before him. The boy never took his eyes off Chata, even as his mother grabbed his hand and tried to pull him away. Chata wondered if the boy had a father, and wondered what kind of father he himself would be. He wasn't sure he would be a good one, and was quite sure he didn't want to be a leader of the tribe. He didn't even want to be a man at this point. He wanted to go back in time and be a boy, like the one disappearing into the crowd, with no worries and no responsibilities. The boy peeked back through the sea of people and smiled at Chata.

Chata smiled back.

***

Nearing the end of the presentation of the gifts, the late summer sun began to set and the sky transformed into shades of pink and red. Once the line of gift givers had ended, Chata and Chiksa approached the altar. Chiksa lit a pipe carved into the shape of a wolf. He drew deeply on the pipe and handed it to Chata. Chata took his turn inhaling the smoke, and together they laid the pipe on the altar as if sharing it with their father one last time. When they returned to their place in front of the crowd, the drums began their hypnotizing rhythms, slowly at first. The tempo increased as eight bare-chested men wearing only loincloths stepped forward and hoisted the coffin onto their shoulders. They walked up the slope to the burial mound, pacing each step with a beat of the drums. When they reached the top of the hill, they turned the box in a circle, ensuring the chief's head was pointed toward the east. They carefully set down the box on the ground and the drums instantly ceased. Even with the thousands of people gathered, the air was completely silent.

After a few moments, a native flute began its melancholy song. The haunting melody escorted a dozen more men as they approached from the sides of the mounds, walking in two lines, carrying torches above their heads. One by one, they tossed their torches onto the box. The dry wood started to smoke, and then with a whooshing sound, the coffin was ablaze. The golden flames glowed against the darkening cobalt sky.

The wistful music continued under the prayers of the high priest, accompanying the smoke that rose into the air, and the people watched as their chief became one with the gods of the sun, the moon, and the stars, and the gods of the rain and the harvest.

Chiksa felt the heat of the flames on his face. He whispered to Chata, "I hope we lead well and Father is proud."

Chata stood with his arms hanging at his sides, a tear rolling down his cheek. He didn't respond to his brother as he watched the billowing smoke.

Salina spoke softly. "You will both be great leaders."

Mia nodded in agreement.

Chapter 3

The Search Begins

Sheriff's deputies were already on the scene when Sheriff Miller arrived. He climbed out of his squad car and pulled a handkerchief from his pocket. He looked around as he unfolded the handkerchief and patted the sweat from his brow. There was no place on Earth as hot and humid as Mississippi in August, and the humidity was growing. Perhaps a storm was in the making. They could use a good rain, but not right now. He needed his men to move quickly before any clues were washed away. There were dozens of uniforms on the scene. Deputies from different departments had swarmed the place. Most he recognized, some he didn't. His eyes fell upon one of his own deputies, the one who always took on missing-persons cases. This deputy had an uncanny knack for understanding exactly what had happened at the scene of a crime. He was always calm, meticulously examining evidence, methodically leading investigations. Today, the man's face was ashen, his eyes dark and troubled. He locked eyes with the sheriff and shook his head slowly, indicating the scene was not a good one. This deputy was the smartest man on the force. If he was visibly concerned, then something was dreadfully wrong at this scene.

The sheriff already knew from phone calls that this was not a drug-related event or a kidnapping. There were no parents involved in a bitter divorce, no vagabonds, no teenagers playing pranks. Usually the parents were the culprits, but this couple—a lawyer and a stay-at-home mom—had already been checked out and neither had even as much as a speeding ticket. They paid their bills on time, attended church, and according to their neighbors, they took good care of their children. She volunteered at the local library; he generously supported the Boys and Girls Club. There were no indications that led the sheriff to think these folks had anything to do with the disappearance of their daughter. But if not the parents, then who? After twenty years in law enforcement, he knew there was always a logical explanation.

He crammed the handkerchief into his pocket, tucked in his wrinkled shirt, and walked toward the deputy. "Is that the father? The blond man wearing the Rolex?"

The deputy nodded toward a man who was leaning against the trunk of a newer model, blue Mercedes, speaking to another deputy. The man's face was pale, his eyes puffy. He kept running his fingers through his hair, his Rolex flashing in the setting sun.

Rich or not, no one deserved this. What if this had happened to Miller's daughter? He always set his personal feelings aside when working on a case, but he found that task difficult when working on anything involving children, especially abused or missing ones. He'd once lost his daughter on a hiking trip in the Tombigbee National Forest. She was missing for only about ten minutes, but they were the most horrifying ten minutes of his life. He couldn't imagine how frightened this man must be right now. Miller pulled his shoulders back to steady himself, or maybe to look like a person deserving of being in charge, and headed toward the father.

"Mr. Speedwell?" He reached out to shake the man's hand, ignoring the deputy standing there. "I'm Sheriff Miller. Can you tell me what happened here?"

Speedwell nodded as he shook hands, making eye contact but not for long. He was preoccupied with the area behind the sheriff, where an ambulance sat on the far side of the parking lot. "I already told your deputies. My wife and I were hiking with our girls when one of them disappeared."

"What do you mean, 'disappeared'?"

Speedwell looked at the sheriff like he didn't understand the question. "Disappeared. Vanished. One moment she was there, the next she was gone. The girls were running up the hill together in front of us. Emily returned alone."

"Returned from where?"

Speedwell pointed toward the mounds. "The other side of that hill."

"How long were they out of your sight?"

Speedwell shook his head. "Maybe a minute or two." His eyes filled with tears. "We searched the whole area, but she was simply…" His voice cracked. "She was simply…gone."

"Emily is your other daughter?"

Speedwell nodded.

"What did Emily say happened?"

"She won't speak. I guess she's traumatized." Speedwell nodded toward the ambulance.

Miller turned and looked into the back of the open ambulance. Its flashing lights were still spinning silently on the roof, red streaks dancing across everything in their path. Inside was a small figure lying on a stretcher, and Miller recognized the paramedic attending her. Standing outside the ambulance doors was a sobbing woman.

"Is that your wife, sir?" Miller asked.

"Yes. Margaret."

"All right, let me speak with your wife and daughter and I'll be back in a few minutes."

Miller walked toward the ambulance's flashing lights, feeling as if he was swimming through swamp water. With each step, the ambulance seemed farther away. He always had this sensation around here. Something about the area surrounding Bynum Mounds and Witch Dance was not right, and Miller's logical mind couldn't fathom what it was or why he couldn't figure it out. This certainly wasn't the first strange incident he'd experienced here. Weird occurrences happened frequently, some due to overactive imaginations and weekend six-packs, and some were unexplainable, but they never before involved a missing child.

After feeling like he had waded a mile through delta marshland, he reached the crying woman.

"Mrs. Speedwell?"

She nodded and wiped her tears with her hands.

Her jet-black hair was tied in a loose bun. She was thin, had manicured nails, expensive gold bracelets, and a huge diamond on her ring finger—a typical rich man's trophy wife. She was probably stunning on a normal day, but her red-rimmed eyes accentuated her fine lines, and at the moment she looked haggard.

"Ma'am, I'm Sheriff Miller. May I ask you a few questions?"

She nodded again, glancing inside the ambulance at her daughter.

"Is this Emily in the ambulance?"

"Yes," she sniffled.

"And your other daughter's name is?"

"Sarah. They're twins."

"Can you tell me about the moment Sarah disappeared?"

"It's all my fault. I took my eyes off them for one minute. One stupid minute."

"Please explain exactly what happened."

She took a breath. "The girls ran over that hill." She pointed at the same hill the father had indicated. "We were right behind them. A few moments later, Emily came back alone."

"That's it? Emily didn't tell you what happened on the other side of the hill?"

"No. She fainted on the top of the hill on her way back. She was only out for a moment. I saw her collapse and by the time I got to her, she was already trying to sit up. I looked around for Sarah but she wasn't there. I called her and called her but she didn't answer. Thomas ran over the hill to search for her but he couldn't find her. I stayed with Emily. I kept asking Emily where Sarah was, but she wouldn't answer me. She kept looking over her shoulder like she was afraid of something. She was pale and shaking. We called 911 and they put her in the back of the ambulance. She hasn't said a word since." Margaret looked back into the ambulance and wrapped her arms around herself.

"Did you hear anything while the girls were out of your sight?"

She shook her head. "Nothing."

"Did you see anyone else out here at the mounds?"

"No, there was no one else here. We actually

commented that we were surprised ours was the only car in the parking lot."

He nodded as he watched her. She was telling the truth. He looked back at the husband, who was still speaking with the deputy. He was telling the truth, too. So, what had happened to their little girl? Miller looked back at Mrs. Speedwell and gestured toward Emily. "May I speak with her?"

Margaret paused, then nodded. "Be gentle with her."

"I will, ma'am."

He climbed into the ambulance and nodded at the paramedic as he sat down next to the little girl. "Hi, Emily. I'm Sheriff Miller and I'm going to help find your sister. Can you tell me anything at all about what happened to her?"

Emily stared straight ahead, not giving any indication she even knew the sheriff was next to her.

"Emily? Do you know where Sarah is?"

Emily's eyes grew wider and her face distorted in fear, but she didn't look at the sheriff.

"Sheriff, I don't know if this is a good idea right now," the paramedic said. "We just got her calmed down. Maybe you could wait until morning to speak with her?"

The sheriff knew waiting until morning wasn't in Sarah's best interest, but realized Emily wouldn't be of any help at the moment. And he trusted the paramedic's judgment. Miller nodded, sighed, and slapped his hands on his knees as he rose and climbed out of the ambulance.

When his boots hit the ground, he said to Margaret, "Okay, ma'am. We'll find your daughter. She can't be far." He started to walk away.

"It's getting dark, Sheriff," Margaret called.

The sheriff turned back.

"Sarah's afraid of the dark."

He looked at the sky, then back at Margaret, and gave her his best reassuring smile. "I'd better get busy, then, ma'am."

He turned away. It would be dark very soon, and many thought this place was haunted. According to reports, there were things in this place that came out at night, things a little girl shouldn't have to face. He needed to get his men moving quickly.

Lori Crane

Chapter 4

Birth and Death

Salina cried out in agony as her baby emerged into the world. Even in the chilled night air, sweat dripped from her forehead, and one of the women wiped her brow with a soft piece of deerskin. When she finished, the woman rose to her knees to see over the heads of the women who were attending the babe.

"It's a girl," the medicine woman said softly.

Salina was overjoyed. Her tears flowed, and the young woman next to her wiped them with the same deerskin as before. "It's a girl," the woman repeated to her.

Salina lifted her head and looked toward the women tending her child. She knew Chiksa would be pleased to have a healthy daughter. The child would be a wonderful beginning to their large family, and they would have a son next time. Salina sighed and rested her head back on the rabbit-skin pillow. A shiver coursed through her body. "I'm cold," she said.

The young woman placed a deerskin on top of her and tucked it in around her.

"Thank you." Another shiver racked Salina's body.

The woman held a gourd to Salina's lips. "Drink."

The hot liquid felt good on her throat. It was sweet and thick and comforting. When the warmth reached Salina's stomach, she relaxed and closed her eyes, finally resting after the long birth. A few moments later, she shivered a third time.

The woman covered her with a second deerskin.

The only thing she had to worry about now was how to be a good mother and raise a beautiful daughter. A wave of joy rushed over her.

A shiver hit her for the fourth time, this time shaking her to her core. She expected the young woman to do something else to comfort her, but nothing happened. She opened her eyes. The woman was ignoring her, watching what was happening at the foot of the bed. Salina looked around the room, which was lit by a dying fire in the corner. The half dozen women who filled the room were important ones, entrusted with the birth of the firstborn heir to the tribe. They were all looking at the same place, intensity on every face. Salina raised her head and looked toward the medicine woman.

"Someone stoke the fire," she heard one of the women say.

The only sound after that was a log being placed on the fire, hissing and popping. Salina realized there were no tears of joy, no wishes of congratulations. The women had not handed her the child. The babe was not crying.

"Why isn't she crying?" Salina asked.

No one looked at her or answered. They scurried quietly on the floor near the foot of the cot as the fire came back to life, filling the room with a yellow glow.

"She has no breath," the medicine woman said.

"No breath? What do you mean, no breath? Let me see her! Give her to me!"

The medicine woman rose, cradling the babe, and walked toward Salina. "No breath," she said as she knelt and placed the infant in Salina's arms.

Salina clutched the babe as if someone would try to take it from her. She moved the rabbit pelt away and roughly rubbed the infant's blue skin as she spoke to her. "Wake up, little one. Cry for your momma." She rubbed harder. "Wake up!"

The women gathered around her, each perfectly still as if moving would make the horrible event even worse. They held in their tears as they listened to Salina speak to her daughter. Salina's tone became louder, more demanding, even angry. When the words turned to rage accompanied by tears, the medicine woman removed the babe from Salina's arms. Salina screamed at her. "Do something!"

A few women tried to calm Salina—rubbing her hand, swabbing her forehead—but she slapped their hands away. She weakly pulled herself up to a sitting position, and between sobs, she begged the women to make her child breathe.

***

Chiksa had waited outside the hut for hours, questioning every woman who entered and exited, but he received no information. He could hear his wife inside crying and yelling something, but he couldn't make out what she was saying. Had she given birth yet? Was she in pain? No one had entered or exited for quite some time. He longed to see his wife, but entering the hut would be highly inappropriate. An owl repeatedly hooted in the distance and tree frogs filled the night with their demanding songs. When the coyotes began their howl, it drowned out all the other night sounds. He couldn't hear much through the thick mud walls so he occupied himself by pacing back and forth in front of the hut. Occasionally he stopped and leaned his ear to the flap door. Salina sounded upset, bordering on hysteria.

A young woman emerged from the hut, nearly bumping into him.

"What is happening?" he asked.

She looked down and hurried away without a word.

He demanded she stop, but she was already out of sight. Someone needed to tell him something soon. He resumed pacing. The coyotes continued howling.

After a short time, the old medicine woman came out, holding a bundle of rabbit fur closely to her chest. She didn't see Chiksa in the dark shadows waiting near the hut and walked right past him.

"Stop!" commanded Chiksa.

She stopped and turned to face him.

"What is in your arms?"

The woman looked down. "The infant. It was born without breath."

Suddenly Chiksa felt without breath also. His knees weakened, and the ground felt like a bog. He took one step toward the woman, then another, unsure if his legs would hold him.

The woman didn't move.

Chiksa reached toward the bundle and watched his own calloused hand move, but it seemed detached from his body. It didn't even look like his hand. 'Without breath' echoed in his head.

She relaxed her hold so he could unfold the rabbit skin.

He pulled back one layer, then another. In the light of the full moon, he saw the perfect little face, and froze. This couldn't possibly be his child, but what other child could it be? It wasn't moving. He looked into the old woman's eyes, scanned her face to see if she was truthful.

She nodded solemnly.

He pulled back the rest of the pelt. A perfect but lifeless form lay in the wrappings. A perfect face, perfect little fingers, perfect toes. Why is she not breathing? This couldn't be happening. Death seemed to be swirling around him. First his father, now his child. Who else would the gods take from him?

"Salina?" he said with a gasp.

"She's all right. She lost a lot of blood and is rightfully very upset, but she'll heal. There will be more children."

Chiksa sighed in relief. He couldn't live without his beautiful Salina. "When can I see her?"

"She'll see you shortly," the old woman said as she recovered the babe and turned to walk away.

Chiksa looked up to the stars scattered across the sky. Why did the gods take his child? Was it something he did? Something Salina did? He didn't know what happened to a person's spirit after death, but he hoped his child was in the arms of his father.

After the old woman disappeared from sight, he walked back to the hut, sat on the dry ground against the mud wall, and wept.

Chapter 5

Rich Martin

The sheriff had called in Search and Rescue as soon as the missing child was reported, and the group was already on the scene. They sectioned off large areas of land behind the mounds and searched all night, but by morning they hadn't found any trace of Sarah Speedwell.

The local radio and television stations had spread the word about her, and as soon as the sun rose, volunteers began flooding the Bynum Mounds. By 7:00 a.m., at least two hundred volunteers had joined the search, covering up to a mile in all directions. The day crept by with no leads. By evening, everyone wondered whether or not the child was still in the area.

Most volunteers suspended their search at nightfall, but this involved a six-year-old child so no one wanted to give up. More than twenty-four hours had passed; time wasn't on her side. The searchers continued to comb the area throughout the second night, using flashlights and floodlights, wading through waist-high weeds, stepping over fallen trees and stumps. Search and Rescue had brought in search dogs trained in wilderness tracking, but after hours with no results, they allowed the dogs to sleep.

The sheriff sat in his office at his computer the entire second night, drinking coffee and clicking through page after page of offenders in his county. He had spent the afternoon at the hospital checking on

Emily, but the child still wasn't speaking. Speedwell's parents had come in to stay with the girl, but interviewing them didn't help the investigation, either. He hadn't slept in nearly forty-eight hours. There had been no trace of the girl past the other side of the hill where she supposedly disappeared. He knew only one thing for certain. Whatever happened to her, she didn't walk; she was carried. He rose from his desk at 4:00 a.m. and poured himself another cup of coffee. He sat back down to search for known child predators in neighboring counties.

As the sun rose on the third day, he drove back out to the mounds and found exhausted people who still hadn't found the slightest hint of what happened to Sarah Speedwell.

That morning, the national news crews descended en masse upon Bynum Mounds and Witch Dance campground. There was no new information to give them. As Mr. Speedwell said in previous interviews, "She simply vanished."

The local and regional news had initially reported basic information: the family was an upper-class household from nearby Nashville on a weekend camping trip at Witch Dance. He was a trial lawyer. She was a former lawyer, now a stay-at-home mom. Their two girls were twins who had just started the first grade.

When the national news reports surfaced, the stories changed from a happy family with a missing child to malicious allegations against the parents, the grandparents, their neighbors, persons who'd lost a case in court against Thomas Speedwell, and anyone else who would make for a good story. Happy families didn't make for good ratings, even with a missing child.

At dawn on day three, Bynum Mounds had

been blocked off by the police, so the reporters surrounded Witch Dance, searching for the Speedwells, whose belongings were still at the campground.

A few hours before the police barricade was set up at Bynum Mounds, following no sleep and no leads, Margaret and Thomas had driven back to the campground and crawled into their tent to sleep for a few hours. They woke to the sound of reporters outside their tent. They emerged to microphones and cameras in their faces, and Thomas escorted Margaret to their nearby car.

"Margaret, what did you do to your daughter?" one reporter yelled.

Margaret sobbed.

Thomas helped her into the car and sped out of the campground onto the main road. "Don't listen to them. They're like a bunch of vultures trying to find a carcass to eat."

"When did they become so mean? I thought they were here to help."

"I don't know, but it's completely unacceptable."

The couple rode in silence for a few miles.

"I want to find Sarah and go back home. This is a nightmare."

"I know. We'll find her. The sheriff is working on it." He turned at the next pull-off and found it vacant. He put the car into park and turned toward Margaret. "I don't think we should stay at the campground. Why don't we go get a hotel room?"

He waited for an answer but none came. It didn't surprise him. After the girls were born, the decisive lawyer he married had disappeared. Margaret was no longer a warrior who could slay dragons; she had become a shell of her former self. She suffered from anxiety over every little detail concerning the girls, sadness over each miscarriage and stillbirth they'd faced before and since the twins were born, and depression over life in general. She couldn't even make a simple decision about where she wanted to sleep. As usual, he made the decision for them. "We'll go stay in Tupelo. I'll find us a room near the hospital so we can be near Emily. Why don't you crawl in the back and sleep for a while? I'll book a room and drive back to the campground and get our things."

"Get the closest room you can. I don't care if it's the worst place ever. I can't stand the thought of being far away, and I certainly don't want to stay in a luxurious resort while Sarah's out in the woods, afraid and alone."

"Okay, I'll do that." While she climbed into the back and tried to get comfortable, he pulled out his phone, but he couldn't get any service. He looked in the rearview mirror at her. She had a sweatshirt rolled in a ball under her head, her eyes closed. He'd wait until she dozed off. He decided to go back and get their things, then drive toward Tupelo and find a room.

It didn't take more than a couple minutes before he heard her softly snoring. She was exhausted. He was, too. He pulled back onto the main road and headed back to Witch Dance. When he arrived, he avoided the crowded parking lot and took the gravel utility road to the back of the campground. Cars weren't allowed to drive into the campground, only bicycles and horses, but this wasn't a normal circumstance. He didn't care if he got a ticket. He glanced in the back. The bumpy road didn't wake Margaret, and he was glad. She needed to rest.

He put the car into park but left it running as he cleaned out their tent. He packed their belongings into the trunk, leaving the tent where it stood, and settled back into the driver's seat. He looked back at Margaret. Still asleep. He was happy to let her rest and happy the mob of reporters had obviously taken a break. He knew they were all back at the entrance of the campground awaiting his return. With any luck, they would stay there. He sighed, suddenly feeling the fatigue of the last few days. He could use a moment of rest himself. He took a light blanket from their tent and wedged it into the driver's-side window to darken the car a bit. He then pulled out his cell phone to search for the nearest hotel. Still no service. He frowned. Why did he ever let her talk him into coming to this back-hills nightmare? What kind of place had no cell service?

She'd wanted to come. She said Mississippi was her roots, and she wanted to share it with the girls. They'd been about an inch away from divorce, and he needed to do something to save their marriage, so he agreed to come here for the weekend. This was supposed to be fun, the start of a new life, a brighter future. He closed his eyes. This was not what they had planned.

His thoughts moved to Emily. As soon as they got to a hotel, he would call his mother to see how Emily was doing. His parents had driven down as soon as they got the news and were staying at the North Mississippi Medical Center with Emily. He hoped the reporters weren't hounding them as well. He trusted his mother to keep Emily safe, but he should probably call the sheriff to see if they could post someone at Emily's room. He wasn't thinking clearly and knew he should make a list of all these phone calls he needed to make, but he had to close his eyes for just a minute. He immediately felt himself floating into sleep.

***

In the parking lot at the entrance of the Witch Dance campground, a dozen reporters huddled, steam rising from their coffee cups, around a white television news van with the black letters WTVA CHANNEL 9 painted on the side. The WTVA reporter spoke loudly to her cameraman, barking orders about the best angle and lighting they would use once the Speedwells returned to the campground. The newspaper reporters watched the snapping television reporter with amusement. They were often in the presence of bossy journalists, but this lady was exceptionally loud and pushy.

One of the newspaper reporters at the scene was Rich Martin from nearby Tupelo. He wasn't interested in the media circus; he was there to help. He felt sorry for the Speedwells, even more so if they had to face this woman. He stood at the back of the crowd and listened to the other reporters discussing the story and sharing information. A few moments ago, while they all had been jockeying for position and establishing their pecking order, Rich had seen the Speedwells return to the campground and sneak up the utility road in their blue Mercedes. He sipped his lukewarm coffee, wondering if he should wait them out or follow them and get the story he came for.

After a while, he dropped his Styrofoam coffee cup in the nearest trash can and casually strolled away, heading in the direction the Mercedes traveled. When he discovered the car parked in the trees in the back of the park, he approached it and knocked on the blanket-covered window. He knew he would ask the same questions that had already been asked by every police officer and every reporter on the scene, but he wanted to hear the answers himself.

The driver cracked the window and started to say something, but Rich cut him off. "Mr. Speedwell, I'm Rich Martin from the *Tupelo Journal*. May I talk with you for a few minutes?"

Margaret woke at the sound of a rich baritone voice. It sounded very familiar and she sat straight up. She looked out the crack at the top of the window and saw the brown eyes of her dearest childhood friend. "Rich?"

Rich leaned into the car to get a better look. "Maggie? Is that you?"

Margaret opened the back door and climbed out of the car. "Oh, my goodness, what are you doing here?"

Rich held out his hands for Margaret to take. "What am I doing here? What are you doing here?" She didn't answer. She wrapped her arms around his neck and hugged him. When she released him, she turned to her husband, who had also emerged from the vehicle. "Thomas, this is my old friend, Rich. We grew up together in Tupelo."

Thomas shook his hand. "It's good to have a friend here. It's getting a bit overwhelming with all these policemen and reporters and search people. It's just chaos."

Margaret was so happy to see her old friend. Rich was an honest man. His bright brown eyes sparkled with warmth. She hadn't ever seen his hair this long. His overgrown curls made him look like an old-fashioned newspaper geek from the fifties who belonged in a smoky room with a pencil behind his ear, typing on a vintage Royal typewriter with a bottle of Wite-Out close by. If he used a pocket protector, Margaret wouldn't be surprised.

Rich turned to Margaret. "Wait! The missing girl is yours?"

Margaret nodded, tears flooding her eyes.

"Oh, I'm so sorry. I've seen the reports and even your family's picture, but I didn't realize it was you! I know there's been an AMBER Alert issued, and I saw the roadblocks when I drove in. Perhaps I can help by getting AP to pick up the story, and maybe pressure from the citizens will get the FBI interested in helping."

Thomas nodded eagerly. "Anything that'll help. We're worried sick."

"I'm sure you are. I bet they've already started going door-to-door. Did they ask you to take a polygraph yet?"

Margaret grimaced. "Why would they do that?"

Rich shrugged. "Maybe they won't. In my years in journalism, I usually see them ask the parents to take a polygraph within the first couple days."

Thomas shook his head. "No, they haven't asked us to do that."

"Well, then, they probably believe you."

"You seem to know exactly how this works," Thomas said.

"I've been a reporter a long time." He smiled, but Margaret and Thomas didn't smile back, so he quickly added, "If you'd grant me an interview, I'm sure I can help."

"Yes, yes, we can do that," Margaret said.

They climbed back in the car, with Rich and Margaret sitting in the backseat, and Thomas twisted around in the driver's seat.

When Margaret and Thomas finished telling their story, Rich asked, "Where is Emily now? Has she said anything?"

Margaret shook her head. "As far as we know she hasn't spoken. She's in the hospital. They admitted her right away, and Thomas's parents are there with her."

"Does anyone else know this?"

Margaret shook her head. "Just the police, I guess. Why?"

"I know these reporters. If they found out your daughter is at the hospital, they're probably camped out there, too."

Thomas frowned. "I thought about that and wanted to call the sheriff and ask him to make sure someone is posted at the hospital. My mother hasn't called us yet this morning, so I assume they haven't been bothered." He glanced at his phone. "Then again, I don't have any service around here so we may have missed her call." He held his phone up in an attempt to get at least one bar. Nothing. "It's almost eight o'clock. I imagine the doctors have already been in, so they're probably up." He looked at his wife and back at Rich. "Mr. Martin, would you mind staying here with Margaret for a few minutes? I'd like to walk up to the road and see if I can get a signal."

Rich nodded. "Of course, and please call me Rich."

"Okay, I'll be back in a few minutes." Thomas climbed out of the car and walked up the gravel road.

Rich climbed out of the backseat and called after Thomas. "Mr. Speedwell?"

Thomas turned back.

"I'll help in any way I can."

Thomas nodded and continued walking.

The moment Thomas was out of sight, Rich sat back down. "Maggie, it's so good to see…"

Her eyes were full of tears.

He stopped. "I'm sorry. Are you okay?"

She shook her head. "I'm just overwhelmed…and I'm scared to death for Sarah. She's never been away from me before, and she's out there all alone." She fell against Rich's chest and sobbed, feeling him wrap his arms around her. He rocked her as she cried. For a few short moments, she felt safe in his arms.

After she composed herself, she pulled away from him in embarrassment. Her eyes scanned where her husband had disappeared only moments ago. She hoped he didn't witness her being consoled by another man. She felt guilty for clinging to Rich, but at the same time, was reassured by his presence. Rich felt like home, and she hadn't felt that kind of comfort in years.

She looked down at her lap and shook her head. What was coming over her?

Rich cleared his throat.

Margaret looked into his eyes. "I'm sorry. I'm just so emotional right now."

"Don't apologize. It's okay. As soon as your husband comes back, I'll go write this story and help get the word out."

Margaret nodded. "I guess that's the best thing

we can do at the moment."

"Where are you staying? Do you need a place?"

She shook her head. "We're going to go rent a room."

"If you need a place, you could stay with my grandmother."

"Grandma Ivy? Oh, I haven't thought of her in years!"

He smiled. "You know she'd love to see you."

She thought about it for a moment. "I couldn't put her in this position. These reporters are hounding us, and I feel like they're just getting started."

"It would be all right. She's used to reporters."

She looked at him. "I'm sorry, I meant no offense."

"None taken."

"Still, I wouldn't want to bring all this craziness into her life."

"Okay, well, the offer stands if you change your mind."

"That's very kind of you. Thank you."

She couldn't take her eyes off him. He would help, she knew it.

He looked back into her eyes. "Gawd, it's good to see you."

"You, too."

The car door opened, jarring them out of their individual thoughts, and Thomas climbed in. "I can't get a darned signal up there. We'll have to get into town before we can call, I guess."

Lori Crane

Chapter 6

Chata and Chiksa

Following the death of his father, then his daughter, Chiksa fell into a deep depression. But it was nothing compared to what Salina was experiencing. For two weeks following her daughter's death, Salina did not emerge from her hut. She refused to rise from her bed, wouldn't talk, wouldn't eat, and stayed wrapped in her fur hide even though the heat was nearly unbearable. She remained in a fetal position, rocking herself back and forth. She barely slept, and spent her days and nights staring at the mud wall of the hut. When she had cried all the tears she could cry, she began chewing her nails. When there were no more nails, she used the jagged edges of what remained to gouge her wrists. She scratched holes in her flesh that bled, became infected, and oozed with pus.

Chiksa sat with her all he could when he wasn't taking care of his clan. On his most recent visit, he couldn't even get her to acknowledge he was in the room, so he called for the medicine woman to look at her and to bandage her sores. Following the visit, Chiksa and the old woman stepped outside.

"Is there anything you can do for her?" Chiksa asked.

The medicine woman shook her head. "I'm afraid there's nothing wrong with her except melancholy. She is being consumed from the inside by her own sadness. I will do what I can, but I can only heal the physical. I'm not a witch. I can't perform miracles."

"What are you telling me?" Chiksa wouldn't accept the possibility he could lose his wife.

"I'm saying that I will do my best, but I cannot assure you the outcome you wish. I don't know what is going to happen. I fear her will to live has been severely compromised." She looked toward the hut. "Her spirit may already be dead."

Chiksa couldn't breathe.

She continued, "If that's the case, I can do nothing. Death will come if she wishes it." The old woman turned and waddled across the barren courtyard, the fringe on the bottom of her skirt swaying and her moccasins kicking up little puffs of dust with each step.

Chiksa watched her go, wishing to call her back, but understanding she would be of no help. There must be something he could do, someone else he could ask for help. But who? There was no one else in his tribe who could heal the way the medicine woman could. He must look elsewhere.

The gods had seen fit to grant Chiksa with brawn and Chata with vision, but today Chiksa wished for the opposite. He desperately wanted clarity. Why had his child been born dead? Why was his wife deathly ill? He needed to find a way to help her. He wished to sit at her bedside and restore her will to live. He wanted time to mourn the loss of his daughter, to sit and cry at her grave at the mounds. He wanted to do a lot of things he had no time for. His tribe needed care, food, and safety. He had no time for pain or feelings or sadness. He resented Salina's freedom to lie in bed and die. He couldn't even do that. His entire life seemed to be one long chore, one long obligation after another. He had always been told he was a lot like his great-grandfather who'd led the tribe here from Mexico—always the man in charge. Chiksa had grown tired of the never-ending struggle between commitments and feelings. He wished Chata would step up and take the reins and lead their people for just one day.

As evening fell, Chiksa found himself sitting in the field, staring at the burial mound where his father had been laid to rest a little more than a full moon ago. Where only fourteen sunsets ago, Chiksa had laid his infant to rest. He looked up at the twinkling stars and said a silent prayer to the nighttime gods to bless his people and to grant him strength. He prayed to his father for guidance. An owl hooted from a nearby tree, which he took as a sign that his prayers were heard. He wished he could cry, but there were no tears left. He couldn't imagine how he would live if Salina died. She was his life, his world. He had never loved anyone the way he loved Salina, including his own father and brother. Salina was breath to him. Someone had to know the way to heal her melancholy before it killed her, which would in turn kill him.

He heard a faint crunching of leaves in the forest. He listened but did not move a muscle. It was not an animal. The rustling sound was human footsteps. Who would be out here this late? The leaves rustled again. He shifted only his eyes toward the sound, and witnessed a figure emerging from the woods, cloaked in black, hunched, shuffling to the center of the field. Chiksa thought it must be the old medicine woman, but he wasn't sure. After watching for a few minutes, he realized the medicine woman moved much more slowly than this person. No one he knew looked like that...at least he didn't think so. It was hard to tell in the darkness. Chiksa remained motionless and barely breathed.

When the figure reached the center of the field, it stood up straight, as if being pulled upright by a string on the top of its head. As it uncurled, its hands extended to the sides with its palms facing upward, and it grew from what looked like an old hag to a healthy person. As if picked up by the same string, it rose straight up into the air. Chiksa's eyes widened as the figure floated above the earth. A breeze caught the figure's cloak and the edges swirled. A wind intensified, blowing around the figure, slowly spinning it in circles, but there had been no breeze a moment ago. A cloudy vortex formed around the figure, resembling tight circles of light gray smoke from a fire, extending from the ground into the clear heavens above. Even though he was known to be a mighty warrior, Chiksa's hands began to sweat and his heart beat wildly, pounding in his ears. He had seen many things in his lifetime, but never anything like this. What kind of creature was this? When the figure hovered about four feet off the ground, the black cape dropped from its shoulders, floating to the ground like a fall leaf, revealing a woman. A young and beautiful woman. Her skin glowed under the stars as if she were the moon itself, coated in shimmering gold. Chiksa gasped and jumped to his feet.

The figure heard him and instantly returned to the ground. The vortex stopped so quickly, he wondered if he had imagined it. The woman retrieved her cloak, covered her nakedness, and walked toward him.

He couldn't move from his spot. There was no

sense in running.

She covered her head with her hood as she neared him. "Why are you here?" she asked in a cracking voice.

"I came to visit with my father," he said in not much more than a whisper.

She cocked her head. "Your father?" She gestured around with both hands, indicating no one else was there.

He pointed to the mounds. "My father died a short time…"

She held her hand in front of his lips as if to silence him. Her fingers were long and bony, covered in deep wrinkles. Her nails were yellowed claws. This was not the beautiful young form he had witnessed only moments ago.

"There is great pain in this place," she said.

"My people have recently lost their chief."

"No. No people. Pain in you." She pointed to his heart, her finger only inches from his chest.

He said nothing.

"Sa…lee…Salina?" she said slowly, her head cocked as if listening to something only she could hear.

"My wife."

"A great blackness has taken her."

"Yes."

"She will die."

He shook his head. "She can't."

"She can." She paused and narrowed her eyes at him. "But she can be healed." The old woman looked up at the sky and her cracked lips parted. Small black gaps between what looked like fangs emitted a foul stench that wrapped around Chiksa. Her yellowed eyes twinkled and she nodded toward the sky.

Chiksa didn't move. He didn't know if this creature had put a hex on him or if he was frozen in fear. It didn't matter. She said Salina could be healed. That's all he focused on.

"You can heal her?"

She was still staring at the sky.

He didn't dare ask again. He didn't want to anger her.

After a moment, she looked back at him. "Yes, yes, I can, but all things come at a price. I will decide the price and will be here again on the full moon. You come. Bring her."

She turned away and moved toward the woods. He couldn't say she walked; it was more like gliding, as if she floated just over the ground's surface.

"What is your name?" he called when she reached the edge of the dark forest.

"Oma."

Chapter 7

Alone

"Okay, I'll be there in a few hours." Thomas hung up.

"Be where?" Margaret asked as she emerged from the bathroom, drying her hair with the dingy motel towel.

"I told Mom I'd be home tonight."

Margaret stopped rubbing her hair and stared at him.

He rose from the edge of the queen-sized bed and took a couple of steps toward her. "I know you're not going to like it, and believe me, I don't want to leave, but I do need to go back to work."

She turned without a response, placed the towel on the vanity, and grabbed the blow dryer off the holder on the wall. She flipped her head upside down, the noise from the blow dryer drowning out anything else he might have to say.

He waited for her to finish. Once she'd snapped the dryer back into the holder, he said, "It's been two weeks, Margaret. We've searched every day from dawn until dusk."

She marched past him and plopped onto the threadbare easy chair in the corner of the room, next to the dirt-encrusted window.

He followed her. "The firm has been very understanding and said to take as long as I need, but I can't expect them to continue their generosity indefinitely."

She looked out the window and didn't respond.

He combed his fingers through his hair and sighed. "I have clients. I'm scheduled for court appearances. A lot of people are depending on me."

She said nothing. His thinking that other people needed him more than his own family did at this moment didn't deserve a response.

"Please don't be upset."

"How's Emily?"

"Mom said she's still not speaking, but she's eating okay and has gone back to school."

When Emily was released from the hospital, Thomas had insisted she return home to Nashville with his parents. Margaret was against it, but Thomas made a pretty good argument that they couldn't drag Emily around the wilderness while they searched for Sarah. Thomas spoke with his mother every day, but the only information Margaret had gotten from her mother-in-law was that Emily watched cartoons for hours. She slept, ate a little bit, and was definitely not the happy child they'd come down here with. Margaret couldn't be in two places at once, so she had no idea how to remedy the situation.

"I'm sure it's helped her, returning to her normal life and her school," he said.

"Will it help you to return to your normal life? When you go back to your twenty-four/seven work schedule, who's going to look after Emily? Is she going to stay with your mother?"

"Mom said she would continue to stay at the house with Emily as long as we need her. Both my parents said they want to help."

She looked out the window again.

He waited for her to say something else.

Finally, she said, "I can't go with you."

"I'm not asking you to go with me. I know you don't want to leave. You need to do what you need to do. I can't tell you what to do in this situation."

She kept her eyes on the empty parking lot outside. A bird flew up from the bush across the street. She watched it fly in circles, bouncing from one branch to the next and noticing the low-hanging gray backdrop behind it. The clouds matched her mood. It had been threatening to rain every day for the last two weeks. Maybe today would be the day it actually did. Maybe it would wash away some of this oppressive heat. Dreary rain would just add to the depression. Could anything be more depressing than this disaster? She looked at her husband's car framed by the peeling yellow lines of the parking space. They looked as if they hadn't seen a fresh coat of paint in years. The car, her husband's pride and joy, was covered with red Mississippi mud. This place was as miserable as Margaret felt inside. One daughter was missing. The other still hadn't said a word and could be damaged for life. What was left of her marriage was crumbling. Now Margaret had to choose between her children. Go home to Emily? Stay here and look for Sarah? There was no choice. Even for Emily's well-being, Margaret couldn't fathom the idea of leaving here without Sarah.

She turned back to Thomas, who had moved to the open doorway, holding his duffel bag, still awaiting a response. "I know you need to go back to work, Thomas. Work has always been your number one priority." She heard the poison in her tone and knew she should bite her tongue, but she couldn't imagine how coldhearted he must be to leave his daughter out here alone. "I can't go home with you. I won't leave Sarah alone out in the woods." Her lip quivered but she refused to cry. She was furious with him. Anger and sadness—lately those were the only two emotions she had.

"Margaret, I know you're angry with me. I understand."

"You don't understand anything. Your dear law partners have always been more important to you than me or your children. Don't think I haven't always known that we come second, or maybe even third. That's one thing that's wrong with our marriage. Your priorities are messed up."

She turned back to the window and heard a sigh from her husband. She wished he would fight with her. She could use a good argument about now. Instead, he walked out to the car to put his bag in the trunk. She watched him out the window. When he closed the trunk, he stood still, staring down at it. After a few moments, he headed back toward the room.

"I don't want to argue with you," he said as he entered the door. "I have to go back."

"Do whatever you have to do. Don't let me stop you." She wanted to break the glass in front of her. She wanted to hit him. She wanted to scream.

He picked up his phone charger from the nightstand, then stopped and turned toward Margaret. "I don't even know how to say this out loud, Margaret, but you have to hear it. This is the reality of what we're facing. Sarah has been gone for two weeks. You know in your heart she hasn't survived this long by herself. Either someone has her or she's…" He couldn't say it.

"She's not dead!" Margaret screamed and jumped up from the chair. "She's not! How dare you even say such a thing!"

He took a step toward her but she turned from him. He dropped his charger on the bed and placed his hands on her shoulders. He softly rubbed them while she sobbed. He tried to not break down himself. They'd had their marital problems and hadn't gotten along at all lately. That's why they'd come on this trip, to try to salvage what was left of the feelings between them before they ended up in divorce court.

Neither Thomas nor Margaret could remember the last time they weren't considering divorce. Following the birth of the girls, their relationship had grown more and more strained. For the last six years, they had tried in vain to conceive another child, but with each miscarriage and stillbirth, they began to blame each other for their individual and collective unhappiness. During their last heated argument, Margaret had told him it seemed too late for more children, perhaps too late for their marriage.

Thomas would like to say he'd been surprised by the comment, but he had not been. He'd felt the same way. He had convinced himself he was pulling away from the relationship because he didn't know how to fix it. He was a man who fixed things—a lawyer, a rational man—but he didn't know how to alleviate his wife's debilitating sadness. She'd once been an independent and free-spirited woman, traits he found extremely attractive, but the last few years, she had become needy and emotional and it was driving him mad.

Her behavior was increasingly compulsive and odd. Their last argument, she said she thought he blamed *her* for the collapse of their relationship. Maybe she was right. Maybe he did. She also accused him of not loving her anymore. He never denied the accusation. Somewhere deep down inside, he wondered if she was right about that, too. He only knew he loved her enough to stay with her for now.

Even with the tension between them, he hated to see her so upset. She was his wife, the mother of his children. The word *children* stabbed him in the gut. He was well aware Margaret was more attached to the children than he was, and for the first time, he realized her pain must be more intense than anything he was experiencing. The pity he felt for Margaret at this moment might be the last spark of love he had for her. Maybe it was good he felt this. Maybe he could start rebuilding on this spark. Maybe they would start rebuilding when she returned home to him. He didn't know when that would be. For all he knew, she might never return.

He knew the moment he decided to go back home that Margaret wouldn't go with him. He wouldn't even consider asking. She would never leave here until she found out what had happened to their daughter. Her obsessive behavior, one of the things that drove him crazy, was the one thing he understood at this moment, and he wished he could share the trait.

He said softly, "I know you need to stay, and I wouldn't want it any other way. I'm sorry to leave you, but I have to go back, and maybe Emily will start speaking again soon and we can get some answers. My parents will be there to help. We'll be okay. You stay here and find our daughter."

She sniffled.

"Margaret, you bring Sarah home, okay?"

Margaret wiped her eyes and nodded, not turning to face Thomas. They had spent two weeks in this dump of a motel. It wasn't the Ritz, for sure, but it was as close to the Bynum Mounds as they could get and they were fortunate to find it. They'd spent the entire time there not speaking to each other, not sleeping, simply staring at the walls when they were in the room, talking to reporters and the police when they were out, plodding through overgrown fields and woods around the mounds, and reminding themselves to keep breathing. Though Margaret missed Emily deeply, she was glad her little girl wasn't here to endure this. She hated to admit it but Thomas was right about that. Emily needed to be home with her friends and her toys and sleeping in her own bed, and she needed a parent. Thomas would have to be the one.

When Rich Martin had offered them accommodations at his grandmother's house, Margaret didn't want to intrude on her with all the reporters camping out around them. She turned and watched her husband place his phone charger in his briefcase, and she made a decision. She knew she couldn't bear to sit alone in this depressing dump, waiting for something to happen. She sat down on the bed. "Rich told me we could stay at his grandmother's house. I think I'll call him and see if the offer still stands."

"That's a great idea. Do that." He snapped closed his briefcase.

Rich's grandmother's house had always been warm and inviting. Margaret had very fond memories of staying there as a child. Now that she thought about it, Rich had always lived alone with his grandmother. Margaret didn't know what had happened to Rich's parents, and she'd never thought to ask him.

Grandma Ivy was a warm and kind woman with a lovely home. She always had a pan of corn bread on the stove and a pitcher of sweet tea in the fridge. The small country house was the epitome of southern charm, surrounded by a white picket fence and giant hydrangea bushes. Going to Grandma Ivy's was probably exactly what she needed right now.

"I'll let the sheriff know what's going on and see if Rich will come pick me up," Margaret said as she rose and picked up Emily's left-behind teddy bear from the bed. "I don't think I can stay here by myself."

"I think that's a good idea." He gently took the bear from her. "Call him today and see if the offer still stands." He picked up his briefcase, moved toward the door, and turned back. "I'm only a couple hours away. Call me if anything happens and I'll be right here. I mean *anything*."

"Okay, I will," she said, but wondered if she would. If it was bad news, she wouldn't want to tell him. If it was good news, she probably wouldn't want to share it with him. It seemed the last of their ties had been severed.

"All right. I'm going to go."

Margaret walked her husband to the car. "Tell Emily I said to be a good girl, and that I'll see her very soon. Tell her I'm going to stay here and keep looking for Sarah."

Thomas kissed her on the forehead. "I'll tell her. Call me and keep me updated."

After he climbed in the car, Margaret pushed

close his door. They looked at each other for a moment, neither knowing what to say. She felt the Mercedes jerk slightly as Thomas put the car into reverse. She stepped back, wrapped her arms around herself, and watched the car pull away. She watched it until it was out of sight and nothing was left but a dusty road. She second-guessed her decision, wondering if she should've gone with him when she heard a clicking sound to her left. She turned and saw a reporter in a rusted Oldsmobile Delta 88 snapping pictures of her. These people had come out of the bowels of the earth, surrounding her and Thomas day and night. Didn't they have any respect for privacy? She flipped the guy the bird and went back into the motel room. She locked the door, pulled the drapes closed, and dialed Rich on the motel phone.

"How are you doing, hun?" he asked.

"Not great. Thomas went home. Half of me feels like I should have gone with him. The other half can't bear to leave here without Sarah. I feel like an awful mother no matter what I decide to do. I'm always letting someone down at every turn."

"I can't even imagine how hard this is for you. What can I do?"

"Listen, I was wondering if Grandma Ivy would still be willing to take me in. I hate the thought of staying at this dumpy motel all alone. And there are reporters out here bugging me."

Rich chuckled. "Don't you hate reporters?"

"You know what I mean."

"Yes, I do. I'm teasing you. I'll tell you what, I'll be there within the hour to pick you up. Pack your things. Grandma Ivy is going to be thrilled. She always loved you."

She whispered a thank you through the tears that were welling up and ended the call.

She looked in the mirror at the foot of the bed. She had aged ten years in the last two weeks.

She dialed the sheriff.

"Hello, Sheriff Miller? This is Margaret Speedwell."

"Hello, Mrs. Speedwell. How are y'all holding up?"

"We're okay. I just called to tell you Thomas went home. You can reach him on his cell if you need him."

"I understand. Are you staying here?"

"I'm staying, but I'm not going to stay at the motel. I'm going to Rich Martin's grandmother's house. Do you know where that is?"

"Yes, I certainly do. I've been to out Miss Ivy's place on occasion. Best pecan pie in Tupelo."

"Oh, I forgot how good her pecan pie is. So, I'll be there if you have any news. You can also reach me on my cell phone. I haven't even had it out of my purse lately, but I'll make sure I keep an eye on it in case you call."

"I have your number right here, ma'am. I'll be sure to call you the moment the situation changes."

"Any new leads from the searchers?"

"No, ma'am, I'm afraid not."

"I didn't think so. I knew you'd call if there were any new developments."

"Yes, Mrs. Speedwell, I certainly would call you immediately with any information."

"Okay, thank you. I hope to talk with you soon."

She packed her things, and within the hour,

Rich knocked on the motel door.

Lori Crane

Chapter 8

The Deal

As the full moon reached its highest point in the sky, Chiksa carried his dying wife down to the field where he had seen the old woman. He laid her on the dewy grass in the middle of the field, hoping she was comfortable. She moaned but never opened her eyes. He stroked the side of her face, and after she quieted, he stood.

The night sky was clear, but a fog was forming in the still air between him and the mounds, and soon his view was obscured by a white gauze. He didn't understand where the fog was coming from, but lately he hadn't understood much of anything. He looked up at the full moon which was being embraced by a misty halo. His eyes then followed the dark forest line around to the mounds where his father and daughter were buried. He closed his eyes, blocking out the mounds and the pain that they represented. He couldn't stand the thought of placing his wife there also. Something had to be done to save her, and it had to happen tonight. The fog's dampness rested on his bare chest as he stood. He opened his eyes and again scanned the tree line that was now misty with low-lying fog. The old woman said she would be here on this night of the full moon. She would come, wouldn't she? She had to. He was only a short breath away from losing his wife, and he would do anything to keep that from happening, including putting his trust in a stranger. No matter the old woman's price, he would pay it.

A soft breeze brushed across his shoulders, giving him a chill. The night had been calm only a moment ago. He wondered if the breeze was caused by her. She was near.

He heard a rustling in the trees directly ahead of him. He saw only blackness for a moment, but then the woman emerged from the thick brush. Like the first time he'd seen her, she appeared in a black cloak with the hood covering her head. Also like the first time, she appeared hunchbacked. She ambled toward him while Salina remained sound asleep.

"I see you brought Salina to see me," the woman said as she neared, stretching out the *ee* sound in the middle of the name.

"You said you could help her. Can you?"

The woman cackled. "Can I? Of course, I can. Will I? Well, that's another question. I told you it would come at a cost."

"What kind of cost?"

"It will be a steep price. One I'm not sure you'll be willing to pay."

"I'll pay anything."

At that moment, Salina woke and moaned. She squinted at the woman, as if trying to bring the woman into focus.

The woman gave Salina a crooked grin. "Salina is the one receiving my help. She is the one who must pay my price."

"Who's this?" Salina mumbled.

Chiksa knelt next to her. "Salina, this woman says she can heal you."

Salina looked at the woman. "Who are you?"

"I am Oma. I have great powers that can heal

you. I can bring back your health. I can pull you away from the brink of death. There's only one thing I request in return. My gifts are eternal but they're not free. They come at a steep cost." She looked at Chiksa. "Please leave us for a moment."

Chiksa hesitated, but knew he had no choice. Whatever the woman asked, he would do. He knelt down to speak to Salina. "I'll be right over there," he said. He rose and walked toward the mounds.

Oma knelt on the ground next to Salina, her cloak spreading around her. "I can give you a potion to heal your body and your spirit. Do you want my help?"

"Yes."

"Very well, but you must pay the price."

"What do you want?"

"My request is simple. I want a child, an infant. You will bring me one."

"How can I get you an infant? I just lost my own."

Oma smirked. "You must know someone expecting a child."

Salina stared at her, not comprehending.

Oma said, "Your sister."

"My sister? Mia?"

"She is to deliver any day, correct?"

Salina didn't know what day it was, but the woman seemed to know Mia had not yet delivered. Salina nodded, still confused.

Oma smiled. "Now you're beginning to understand."

Salina realized what the woman was asking of her. "No, no, I can't take Mia's child and give it to you."

"She's having two. She will still have one."

"No, I can't do that."

"If you want my potion, you can." She paused. "And you will."

"There has to be something else I can give you."

"No, there is nothing else I want. A life for a life. Sounds fair, don't you think?"

Salina didn't respond.

"Do you want to live?" the old woman asked.

The field was deathly still and silent, except for the pounding of Salina's heartbeat in her ears. She lifted her head, instantly feeling dizzy and weak, and promptly laid it back down again. If she wanted to live, she had no choice but to give in to the old woman's demands. Death would do nothing but break Chiksa's heart, and she couldn't bear to see him in pain. She needed to live, to give him children, to stand by his side as they led the tribe, to grow old with him and care for him. She spoke slowly. "If you heal me, I will get you the child."

"I thought you would, my dear." Oma clasped her hands together in front of her lips, a wicked smile forming behind them. Her bony, wrinkled fingers had yellowed nails like the talons of a bird of prey. "When you return here with the child, I shall be waiting for you." She reached into the folds of her cloak and produced a small clay vial. She twisted the stopper off with a popping sound. A disgusting odor filled the air. Oma reached a cold hand under Salina's head and held the vial to Salina's lips. "Drink."

Salina swallowed, grimacing at the potion's

bitter taste and stench.

The woman returned the top to the vial and placed it back in her cloak. "You will be well by morning. When you return with my reward, our dealings will be finished."

Salina laid her head back on the ground and closed her eyes.

The next thing she felt was her husband picking her up. She rested her head against him, feeling the comfort of his warm shoulder.

"Where did she go? Are you all right?" he asked.

Salina moaned but didn't answer. She slept.

Lori Crane

Chapter 9

Grandma Ivy

Rich pulled his old Lincoln onto his grandmother's gravel driveway.

"The house hasn't changed at all," Margaret said. "The hydrangea bushes are still here. The picket fence around the garden is still just as I remember." Albeit it could use a fresh coat of paint, she thought. The ranch-style house had a covered front porch running the entire length of the facade. There were two front doors, one on the left that led directly into the living room, and one on the right that opened into a foyer. Margaret remembered the house well. Behind the living room was the master bedroom that Margaret had never entered as a child. Behind the foyer was a hallway that led to the kitchen and dining area in the back of the house. Three doors on the right side of the hallway led to two small bedrooms and a single bath between them. Margaret had always thought it a strange layout for a house. How would a guest know which front door to knock on? The porch looked as if it had recently seen a fresh coat of paint and was just as Margaret remembered, including the old rocking chairs and the lush green ferns that hung around the edges. Large white hydrangea blossoms lined either side of the front porch.

In contrast to the emerald leaves of the ferns and hydrangeas, the rest of the front lawn was brown and barren; not a blade of grass grew on this property. Four giant pecan trees shaded the yard with nothing but dirt embracing their feet. Margaret remembered laughing at the yard as a child. What kind of front lawn had no grass? Well, at least it made for easy gathering of the pecans that fell from the trees every fall. As children, Margaret and Rich used to fill bucket after bucket with them, and Grandma Ivy baked the most delicious pecan pies Margaret had ever tasted until this day.

"The hydrangeas are beautiful when they first bloom. Tend to fade this time of year, I'm afraid. Too hot for them to stay vibrant, I guess." Rich got out of the car and walked around to Margaret's side.

When he opened the passenger door, the scent of pine trees filled Margaret's nostrils. The smell of her childhood. A row of pines lined the driveway on her side, casting dancing shadows on the ground below. Margaret couldn't believe the trees were still standing. They looked the same, towering above the driveway. She remembered her mother complaining about the sap that splattered the hood of her car every time they visited. She hated those pine trees, but Margaret loved them. Margaret loved the smell of them, the cones that littered the ground, and the dried needles that gathered around the trunks. She climbed out of the car and turned around and around, taking in the property. An old split rail fence ran behind the pines, running from the road all the way down to the barn, which still stood tall and proud and had to be four or five acres away. She couldn't believe how beautiful that old red barn still was. Chickens milled around the edge of the vegetable garden at the foot of the drive just behind the picket fence. A small pond glistened in the distance. There used to be white geese who lived near the pond and ducks who swam there. She was sure they would be long gone, but everything else was exactly the same, precisely the way Margaret remembered it.

Before Rich could get Margaret's bag from the backseat of the car, there was a slam of the screen door. Margaret turned toward the house and saw Grandma Ivy treading across the covered porch, her hand over her brow, blocking the glare of the afternoon sun.

Grandma Ivy's pale, translucent skin was like something from an Ivory Soap commercial, her hair glowing snow white. Margaret thought of corn bread and sweet tea for the first time in years and it made her smile. A soft breeze blew across Margaret's face, sweet relief from the blistering heat, and the wind chimes at the far end of the porch tinkled. Another memory. A black cat rubbed Grandma Ivy's legs as she reached the edge of the steps.

"Grandma Ivy, I've brought Maggie to stay for a while," Rich called from the driveway.

"That's wonderful," the old woman replied, clasping her hands together. "Come up here, dear. Let me get a good look at you. You look grown."

"I am grown, Grandma Ivy."

From the looks of it, Grandma Ivy hadn't changed any more than the property. She still wore a full apron with some faded fruit design on it, a knee-length dress underneath, and support hose with clunky black shoes. She could have come straight out of the sixties—or maybe the thirties; Margaret wasn't familiar with the fashions of the decades. Either way, it had been at least twenty years since Margaret saw this woman posed this same way in these same clothes on this same porch. Margaret felt a great sense of nostalgia as she headed toward the porch. She didn't know Grandma Ivy's age, but the woman had to have been one hundred back in the day. That would make her about one hundred twenty now. No, that couldn't be. Margaret made a mental note to ask Rich about it later.

Grandma Ivy shooed the cat away and stepped down one step, then another, and Margaret hurried over to keep her from walking the whole distance between them. Grandma Ivy reached for Margaret's hands.

"You poor dear. You've been through such an ordeal."

Grandma Ivy's wrinkled hands were the softest skin Margaret had ever touched. Like silk. Margaret looked into the old woman's eyes, and in their crinkled corners, Margaret felt such compassion and kindness it brought tears to her eyes. Those eyes were the most comforting memory of this place. Those eyes, the color of a cool, cloudy day, seemed to learn every secret of Margaret's soul with one look.

"Oh, don't cry, dear. We'll find your little girl. I promise."

Margaret wrapped her arms around Grandma Ivy's waist and her shoulders relaxed. This place, this woman, offered an overwhelming sense of safety, like Margaret was the lost child who was finally home. This thought caused tears to stream down her cheeks. Grandma Ivy didn't let go. They stood in each other's arms until Margaret finally released her.

"I'm so happy you're here, Maggie, or do they call you Margaret now?"

Margaret smiled. "You can call me whichever you prefer."

Grandma Ivy leaned her head back and looked

through her bifocals. "Well, since you're all grown up now, I guess we should call you Margaret. My, my, look at your beautiful hair. You used to keep it short as a girl, but it's so long now. And that jet-black color has always been what I remember most about you. Rich said your daughters are blondes. How did that come about, dear?"

"Their father is blond. They got it from him."

The old woman patted her on the shoulder. "You'll have to tell me more about your girls and your husband. You ran off and got married, and I'm so far behind on what's going on in your life."

"The only thing going on right now is we're looking for Sarah." Margaret's lip quivered.

Grandma Ivy took Margaret's hand and turned toward the porch. "Everything will be okay now that you're here, Margaret. Let's go inside and I'll pour you some iced tea."

"I'd like that, and thank you so much for allowing me to come stay with you for a while." She wiped her cheek and tried to smile.

"You are always welcome here, my dear. It's been far too long since you've come for a visit. I'm sorry it's under such sad circumstances."

The women walked arm in arm as they chatted, with Rich trailing behind, carrying Margaret's bag. The cool indoor air felt good on Margaret's face. She didn't remember the house having air conditioning in the old days, but she heard the hum of an air-conditioning unit in the living room and was grateful she wouldn't have to endure the Mississippi heat without it while staying in this old house. After her life in Nashville in her big house with her central air, she couldn't remember the last time she complained about the heat.

She followed Grandma Ivy down the hallway, passing the bedrooms and bathroom, and they entered the bright kitchen at the back of the house.

After Rich dropped off Margaret's bag in the guest room, he joined them in the kitchen, where Grandma Ivy was pulling glasses out of the cabinet and Margaret was looking out the window into the back yard. "Have a seat," he said to Margaret, gesturing toward the small round table in the corner. "Let me get those for you, Grandma."

Margaret sat down in the nearest chair and looked around the room. The yellow paint on the old clapboard was faded now, peeling and worn around the corners and the doorjambs, almost in style with the current farmhouse decor. Sunlight streamed through the wavy glass of the old windows, creating a soft, buttery color everywhere. The furnishings hadn't changed, including the round turquoise table with the chrome and turquoise vinyl-padded chairs. This would be called retro now, but it used to be the latest fashion. Life used to be so simple. When she'd sat at this table as a child, not much older than Sarah, Margaret had never imagined being in such an awful situation. She took a deep breath and willed herself to not start crying again.

Grandma Ivy approached the table with the half-full iced-tea pitcher. "Oh, you poor child." She set the pitcher down and grabbed a box of tissues off the top of the refrigerator. She placed them in front of Margaret and sat down. "Now, fill me in. What has happened recently in the search for your daughter? Rich regularly updates me on what's going on out in the world, but he hasn't been home much the last few weeks."

"Home? He still lives here?" She watched Rich fill the glasses with sweet tea and tried to focus on the present, but she was finding that difficult in this nostalgic place.

Rich nodded, his face turning ten shades of red.

Grandma Ivy interjected. "Oh, it's not like he still lives at home, though I don't know what's wrong with that. No, dear, he bought this house from me years ago. So, I guess I live with him, not the other way around. But never mind that. Tell me about your daughter."

Margaret wiped her nose with a tissue. "Well, obviously we're still looking for her." She looked down at the glass Rich had put in front of her and struggled to continue. Should she mention her husband leaving because he had more important things to do? How about the fact Emily hadn't uttered a single word since the incident? Or maybe that her other six-year-old could be lying dead in a ditch somewhere? Margaret ran her finger across the beads of sweat rolling down the glass; they looked like tears. "We don't have any leads to go on at his point. Sarah just disappeared." She couldn't be lost in the woods. They've looked everywhere. Somebody had to have taken her. She lost her train of thought, watching the tears on the glass.

Grandma Ivy cleared her throat and patted Margaret's hand. "You will find her, my dear. You'll keep looking as long as it takes, and you will find her."

Something in Grandma Ivy's tone and gaze was so confident, Margaret felt a shiver run down her spine. Of course, this elderly woman could know nothing of Sarah's disappearance, but something in her tone made Margaret sense that Grandma Ivy could see into the future. If she said Sarah would be found, then Sarah would be found.

They sat in silence for a moment, the only sound coming from the ticking clock above the sink. Margaret took a sip of tea and looked out the window into the sunny yard. A huge weeping willow swept its long branches across the small pond at the far end of the yard, tickling the top of the water. Margaret used to grab those branches and swing out across the water, trying to fly, and splashed into the center of the pond. Rich never wanted to swing on the branches, but Margaret would pester him until he gave in. Back then, she was always the one pushing Rich to do things he didn't want to do, things that usually ended up getting them into trouble, but the memories and the laughs were all worth it. Funny, she hadn't thought about that tree or that pond in decades. The memories in this place were so vivid, it seemed strange they never came to her mind back home. How and why did she push such loveliness so deep down as to never think of it? Was her life so ripe with sadness and confusion now that she forgot how to enjoy life's simple pleasures?

Margaret wondered if Thomas was home yet. Maybe she should call him and check, but she really didn't want to talk to him. The last couple of weeks had been filled with nothing but stress, which had brought out the worst in both of them. Communication in any form with Thomas at this moment would only lead to another argument, and she simply didn't have the strength.

She had to admit to herself this was nothing new. Their marriage had been on shaky ground for six years. She had been trying to have another child since the twins were born, but with each miscarriage, she'd grown unhappier and Thomas more distant. They disagreed constantly about how to raise the children they already had, which was just another collapsing brick in their shaky marriage. Margaret knew she was a controlling and neurotic mother who only wanted to keep her girls safe. Thomas knew nothing. He was never home.

The way the girls ran everywhere always made her nervous. What if they fell? They could scrape a knee, bust a tooth, break a bone. Thomas knew how she felt about their behavior, but he didn't seem to care. In fact, he seemed to encourage them. Sometimes it felt like it was her against all three of them. When she voiced her opinions, Thomas implied they were stupid. He never said as much, but he made his thoughts clear without words. Maybe he was right. Maybe her worry was stupid. She just wished she could encase the girls in bubble wrap. Maybe she would relax a little if she knew they couldn't get hurt. Thomas wanted the girls to be free to make their own choices and decisions, to learn from their mistakes. Margaret was frightened of mistakes.

Maybe trying to have more children was a mistake. Maybe staying together was a mistake.

If she could just get Sarah back, she would take her any way she could, scraped knees and all. The epiphany made her realize maybe the details of her daily life wasn't the thing that needed to change. Maybe she needed to change her thinking. She didn't know if either process would repair her broken relationship with Thomas, though. He always let the girls do what they wanted, and Margaret couldn't tolerate it. If he hadn't allowed the girls to run that day, maybe Sarah would still be here. Margaret pushed that thought away. No, she would not start blaming her husband for what had happened. She realized she wasn't breathing and gasped for air.

"Anyone want some more tea?" Rich shook the ice in his empty glass.

Grandma Ivy began to rise from her chair. "Let me make some."

"No, no, Grandma, don't get up. I can make it."

She sat back down. "Well, if you're sure."

He filled a pan with water and a few Lipton tea bags and placed it on the stove, leaning over to check the flames. "So, Grandma, you haven't seen Maggie in, what, twenty years?"

Grandma Ivy nodded. "Yes, it's been quite a long time, but old souls never lose touch. It's like we haven't missed a day, isn't it, dear?"

Margaret smiled. "Yes, nothing here has changed." She looked at the windowsill next to the table. Framed by a yellow and white gingham valance, the sill housed five little carved figurines. "You even still have those little stone animals. I loved to play with those." Another memory she had forgotten.

"Those animals have been there for a hundred years. Seems like it, anyway. They're made of greenstone, if I remember correctly. Let's see, there's a jaguar, a coyote, an eagle, a bear, and what's the last one?"

"A coiled rattlesnake," Rich piped in as he spooned sugar into the pitcher.

"That one was always my favorite," Margaret said.

Grandma Ivy smiled. "Most people don't like that one very much, but you, my dear Margaret, have never been 'most people,' have you?"

Grandma Ivy was right about the Margaret she

used to know, not so much now. Little Maggie had been a ball of fire, bold and brave, certainly not your average prissy little girl. She was out to conquer the world and had no doubt she could do so. Time had changed everything, yet Margaret didn't know exactly when it had happened. She was now a suburban housewife and had given up her profession and her social life to stay home with her children. She had no hobbies, no visions, not much of a future. She had become "most people."

"Did I ever ask you where you got those?" Rich returned to the table with a fresh pitcher of tea. He sat across from Margaret.

Rich would have rather sat next to her, if only to avoid his grandmother's all-knowing gaze. He was amazed Maggie was back, and she looked more beautiful than he remembered. He had always loved her, had fully expected to marry her once they grew up. But she had run off to college and had not come back. The next thing he heard, she was married, and he gave up on his fantasy and never tried to contact her. He never told her of his feelings, but his heart had been broken for the last twenty years. Seeing her filled him with hopes and desires that his dreams could come true. He knew the appropriate thing to do was to put his love back in the box where he'd kept it for the last two decades, tucked away from everyone, even himself. He was trying to do just that, yet here she was, sitting in his house, drinking his tea. If his grandmother caught him looking at Margaret across the table, she would immediately know what he was thinking and feeling. He couldn't look at her while his grandmother was in the room. Margaret was the only girl he'd ever loved, and the fact she was back was incredible. Even under the current circumstances.

"I think I got those figurines from a childhood friend." Grandma Ivy looked perplexed, as if trying to remember something that was just out of reach. "Yes, I'm certain we had those when we were children. Maybe someone gave them to us. I really don't remember."

"Well, everything here is exactly as I remember it," Margaret said. "This home has always been so warm and cozy." She looked at Rich. "You were lucky to grow up here with your grandmother."

"I certainly was!" He grinned at his grandmother.

"I don't remember if I ever knew what happened to your parents," Margaret said.

"We don't ever talk about it. Never did. I don't really know much, except they were gone before I was old enough to remember anything about them."

Grandma Ivy nodded. "Yes, they were gone before you were six months old, but you were the sweetest little tyke. I couldn't let anyone else take care of you. I was happy to raise you myself."

Margaret watched Rich pour more tea into her glass. "So, what happened to them?"

Grandma Ivy rose from the table. "I need to get some supper on the stove if we're ever going to eat tonight, and that's a long story for another day." She shuffled toward the old farm-style sink.

Rich looked at Margaret and shrugged.

Chapter 10

Salina

Salina woke and looked around the dim room. Her husband was softly snoring, slumped over in a chair by the ashes of last night's fire. She'd had the weirdest dream, something about an old woman in a black robe. She couldn't put her finger on it, but knew she had to get out of bed and do something. Something urgent. She stretched her arms and legs under the fur hide. Her calves were tight; she hadn't walked in a long time. Since the birth of her still-born daughter, Salina hadn't had any desire to rise from bed. The only thing she'd wanted was to die along with her daughter, and for a while, she'd thought she would. Today she felt different. She felt healthy and alive and anxious to get up. Did this have something to do with last night, or was it just a dream?

Chiksa stirred in the chair. They stared at each other, as if waiting for the other to break the silence. Finally, he asked, "How do you feel?"

She smiled. "Better than I've felt in a long time."

He sat up straight. "You do? Do you remember what happened last night?"

She shook her head as she sat up. "I had a weird dream about an old woman."

He rose from the chair and knelt down next to her. He rubbed his knuckles across her temple, moving a strand of hair that had been lying across her cheek. "It was no dream."

"No? There was a woman? Who was she? And, where were we?"

"That woman gave you a potion to make you better."

Salina touched her lips. "Oh, yes, I do remember something. It had a horrible, bitter taste."

"Do you remember what she said to you? What she wanted?"

Salina thought for a moment, trying to piece together the woman, the place, the conversation. It all came rushing back to her. "Yes! She wanted a…" Salina put her hand over her mouth. Did Chiksa know what the woman had asked of her? Should Salina tell him?

Chiksa waited.

Salina glanced around the room. They were alone, but she whispered, "How am I supposed to know when and where to meet her again?"

He spoke close to Salina's face. "She saved your life with her potion. She said her price was steep, and when we return with the item, she'll know. She didn't say when. She simply said when we return to the clearing at the mounds, she'll be there."

"Who is she?"

Chiksa shrugged.

"Maybe she won't show up."

"I'm quite certain she'll be there. She said she'd be there when I brought you there, and she was."

"You saw her there before?"

He nodded. "She just appeared one night. She seemed to know everything about you and offered to help. She told me to bring you to the clearing."

"She's not one of us, right? Not someone from our village or a neighboring village."

"No, she's not one of us. I don't quite know who she is."

Salina looked down at the hide covering her legs and ran her fingers through the soft fur. "I don't think it's possible to pay her price."

Chiksa waited for her to reveal the old woman's demands.

"Maybe we should go there and tell her we can't pay her. It's just not possible," Salina continued.

"But we promised her payment in exchange for the potion."

She looked at him sternly. "Well, we need to tell her we can't keep our promise."

Chiksa shook his head. "I don't think she's the kind of woman who will allow us to back out of a promise."

"What would she do? Kill me?"

Chiksa's face turned pale.

"Would she?" Now it was Salina's turn to be stunned.

Chiksa pulled his shoulders straight. "I don't know what she asked you for, but you will pay it, and we will do as we promised."

She nodded. "Yes, you're right. We promised." Her eyes fell to the black walls of soot inside the fireplace. He didn't know the price, and she would not tell him. It was her burden and hers alone. *A life for a life* came back to her, and suddenly her soul felt as black as the soot on those walls. She had to keep her promise to deliver a child to the old woman. But how?

Salina asked Chiksa to escort her down to the creek to bathe. Except for the previous night's adventure that she barely remembered, she hadn't been outside for weeks. Chiksa helped her dress and walked her into the village courtyard. She felt a little weak and knew it would be overwhelming to have tribe members gather around her, inquiring about her health, so she moved slowly and cautiously, but soon realized it must all be in her head, as her legs felt strong, her head felt clear. She felt well. She could face them if they approached her.

They walked hand in hand through the village square but surprisingly no one approached. The courtyard was deserted. Chiksa saw a young boy scraping a hide at the edge of the courtyard. "Where is everyone?" Chiksa asked.

"The men are hunting, and the women are with Mia. I heard the old medicine woman say she is having two babies. I didn't know that was possible." The boy went about his business, not waiting for another question.

Salina's breath caught in her chest. Today would be the day.

Chiksa heard her gasp and squeezed her hand. The look on her pale face told him the old woman's price had something to do with Mia. But what? Not one of the babies. No. The old hag couldn't possibly demand such a thing.

But if his suspicions were correct, he would be forced to decide between his brother and his wife. Had he already made his decision by promising the old woman anything she wanted? Chiksa would speak with Salina about it later when they were alone.

Salina pulled her hand away from his. "I need to wash then go to Mia's. I'll be fine alone."

Chiksa didn't know how to respond. Stunned,

he watched his wife walk away. He didn't know whether he should go with her or go to his brother's or go ask the old woman what she had demanded. He should do something, but he didn't know what that was. It was not like him to be indecisive.

After a few moments, he slowly turned and walked back to his hut. He sat in his chair next to the fireplace and waited for Salina to return. The hours crept by. He snacked on some figs. He repaired a weak spot in the roof. He sat behind the hut and watched the birds dance in the trees. When night fell, he lit a small fire in the fireplace. Not enough for heat, only for light. Finally, he went to bed alone. He tossed and turned, wondering if he should go looking for Salina. No, she was a capable woman. She would not want him doting over her.

Salina returned just before dawn. The fire had died. The light from the waning moon shone through the small opening in the mud wall. He watched her tiptoe across the room. She took off her shawl and combed her fingers through her hair to loosen her braid. She looked as if she had never been ill and wasn't on her deathbed only yesterday. He watched her for a while, and finally cleared his throat.

"I didn't know if you were sleeping," she said.

"I'm not."

She took off her shoes and crawled onto the cot next to him.

"Well?" he asked.

"It is done," she said without looking at him.

"What happened?"

"I met with the old woman and gave her the payment she requested."

"Did anyone see you?"

"No, I don't think so."

They lay in silence. Chiksa was certain he could hear his heart pounding. He waited for her to drift off to sleep, but her breathing didn't slow. He could feel the tension radiating from her body, and knew his suspicions were right. The payment to the hag was indeed a steep one, one that might destroy everything.

"Was it a boy or a girl?"

"A girl."

Chapter 11

Bynum Mounds

Margaret woke to the smell of bacon. She stretched in the twin bed, feeling more refreshed than she had in a long time. Not only did she feel safe and comforted by the people around her, she felt like she was home again. It was the best sleep she'd had in weeks. Someone was in the kitchen, and she wondered if it was Rich or Grandma Ivy. She heard the faint perk of an old-fashioned coffee pot. Gurgle, perk, gurgle, perk. She hadn't heard that sound in decades.

She pulled the patchwork quilt up to her chin and looked around the room. It was strangely damp in the room and she noticed the window was cracked open. A white vinyl roller shade was pulled down most of the way. She didn't remember pulling it down last night, or whether it had been up or down.

On the other side of the room sat another twin bed with a matching quilt. Margaret was certain the quilts were handmade by Rich's grandmother. Somewhere in her foggy memory, she had a vision of Grandma Ivy sitting in a thread-worn armchair in the living room, glasses resting on the end of her nose, sewing stitch after meticulous stitch while the evening news played on the television. She hadn't thought about it at the time, but now she wondered how Grandma Ivy could see those tiny stitches in the dimly lit room. Margaret couldn't place exactly when that memory was from, but she must've been only eight or ten at the time. She was certain these quilts were the same ones Grandma Ivy had been sewing. They matched the butter yellow walls in the quaint room.

A picture on the wall above the other bed caused memories to come flooding back to her. It was a small painting of a little girl and a little boy walking across a bridge, with an angel hovering, watching over them. Though the girl was bigger than the boy, Margaret had always thought the children in the picture were her and Rich, and the angel was his mother. She knew every detail of that picture—how many times had she seen it to have every aspect memorized? The little girl's dress, the boy's hat, the wooden bridge, the beautiful angel with her enormous white wings. Margaret couldn't remember if she'd slept in this room, but she remembered staring at that picture so it must have happened at some point. The memories were fuzzy, like they were from another lifetime.

She looked back at the window. How long had it been since she'd slept with a window open? Houses were locked up tight now. She wouldn't let the girls sleep with a window open. They would catch cold. Wouldn't they? The girls would love to stay in this room. Why hadn't she ever brought them here for a visit? Why hadn't she come here herself? How could she have created a life so distant that she didn't have time to visit old and dear friends?

She would have to get a copy of that picture for the girls' room. And once Sarah was back, Margaret would let them sleep with the window open. Maybe she hadn't thought of this place because she'd been too busy raising the girls to dwell on the past. Carrying twins had been difficult. Rearing them hadn't proved much easier. Then each day, each month, each heartbreak following another lost pregnancy had made it a struggle for her to stay sane. She'd had to focus on raising her girls to become decent women, suitable wives, and mothers. Her own upbringing with her strict mother in Tupelo had left no room for anything except to become a respectable young lady. Lord knows, she had fought that status quo her entire life, but with her own girls, she'd thought maybe her mother had been right to be so strict. Margaret didn't know anymore. Her mother would turn in her grave if she saw the way young women behaved today. They were too independent, too free. They made too many mistakes at the expense of those around them. They were self-absorbed. Margaret admitted to herself she had been like that too, well, before she had the twins.

She had softened with age, but since she was married to a successful lawyer, she had the option of working or staying home with her children. Of course, she chose the children. She doted on the girls, fretting over each scrape, each vegetable, each nap time, the right kind of laundry soap, the perfect preschool. If the schedule was thrown off for any reason, it would send Margaret into a tizzy, and the way Thomas came and went made keeping the girl's routine even more difficult.

She had attended college up in Tennessee, leaving Mississippi against her mother's wishes. She earned her doctorate and became a lawyer, a good profession for someone with her former boldness. She didn't know if she had it in her anymore, even if she did choose to return to the profession. Many thought a female trial lawyer was unusual and not fitting for a young woman born and bred in the great state of

Mississippi, but Margaret loved being the powerful one in the room who could convince a jury of just about anything. Margaret liked power. Correction: Margaret used to like power. Now, she felt powerless.

After college, she landed a job at a small law firm, and was too busy to return home for more than two days for her mother's funeral. The event deflated Margaret's sails, but she refused to show it. She pushed down the guilt of not coming home more to see her mother. She pushed down the pain of not having been there when her mother died, even though her mother had died suddenly of a massive heart attack. Margaret didn't get to say goodbye. She didn't get to say, "I'm sorry." The weight of the guilt was suffocating. Her poor mother died alone. No child to hold her hand. No husband present, as Margaret's father had left them when Margaret was only an infant. She never knew her father. She remembered the afternoon her mother called her at her new apartment.

"Hi, mom."

"Hi, honey. Listen, I have some bad news. Your father is dead."

"Really?"

"Yes, I'm sorry. I just heard he died in an automobile accident down on the gulf. They said it was a drunk driver. Ran him off the highway."

"Okay, mom. Listen, I have an interview in a few minutes. I have to run. I'll call you later."

She never called her mother back. A month later, she got the news of her mother's heart attack.

Growing up, she was always a loner with few friends, and that never changed. She had never been a social butterfly, but after her mother's funeral, she'd spent most nights alone or in a quiet restaurant with a girlfriend. Within a few short years, all of her girlfriends had married, begun having children, or moved to other cities, and Margaret found herself sitting alone more often than not. A decade of burying herself in her work left her wondering if she'd ever meet a good man to share her life.

One afternoon after a strenuous court appearance, she ran into Thomas, literally, on the cement steps in front of the old courthouse. She was digging into her purse to find her cell phone and crashed right into him. The contents of her purse bounced down the steps, and her favorite lipstick rolled off the curb into a puddle on the street.

Thomas grabbed her arms to steady her.

She'd covered her humiliation by saying he should watch where he was going, but when she saw his face, she stopped in midsentence. He was the most beautiful creature she had ever seen. He watched her with amusement and the slightest cocky grin. His blond hair framed the most exquisite blue eyes Margaret had ever seen. She backpedaled and apologized profusely, blabbering one excuse after the next.

"It's okay. Really. It's all my fault," he said.

She blushed. *Blushing? Really? What's the matter with you?* she thought. She wasn't used to a man gazing at her so intensely, penetrating right into her very soul, and she forced herself to stop talking long enough to stare back. What a beautiful smile he had.

He cleared his throat. "Um, let me help you gather your things."

"No, that's okay. I can do it." She knelt down and began putting her things back into her purse.

"Well, then, at least let me make it up to you by buying you a cup of coffee."

She stopped and stood straight up, gawking at him. She couldn't remember the last time a man had asked her out. Was this a date? This striking man in his impeccably tailored suit and expensive haircut couldn't possibly be interested in her, could he?

"Unless, of course, you have somewhere you need to go. You seemed to be in quite a hurry."

A car revved its engine at the bottom of the steps. She looked down to see the car splash through the puddle and run over her tube of lipstick. She looked back at the striking man in front of her. "No, I don't have anywhere to go—well, not at this moment, anyway. I guess, if you'd really like to, and then apparently I need to stop by the store and buy a new tube of lipstick."

He grinned, and his dimples were dazzling.

She sighed. "I think I need a cup of coffee."

"Well, good. I'd like to buy you one. I'm Thomas." He offered her his hand.

She shook it with one hand while smoothing her hair back with the other. Her hand tingled at his touch. "I'm Maggie."

They married a few short months later.

"As soon as she's up, we're going to the mounds," she heard Rich say from the kitchen.

"Do you think she would mind if I went along?" Grandma Ivy asked.

"No, I'm sure she wouldn't mind, but do you think you can get around all right out there?"

"Well, I'm old, but I'm not that old. I can walk just fine. Slow, but fine."

The sound of their voices jarred Margaret back

to reality, to her missing child, to her current relationship with Thomas, to the whole reason she was here. She jumped out of bed, threw on shorts and a tank top. She couldn't stay under this comfortable quilt, hiding in her memories in this old house.

She tiptoed down the hall to the bathroom and splashed some water on her face and brushed her teeth. The image in the mirror wasn't a beautiful one, but it was as good as it was going to get. She pulled her hair into a high ponytail, examining the right side of her temple. A gray hair. She pulled it out. She pinched her cheeks in an attempt to put some color back into them. With all the time she had spent outside the last couple of weeks, one would have thought she wouldn't look so pale, but lack of sleep, minimal food, and the stress of a missing child were taking their toll. She was beginning to look as bad as she felt.

After a quick breakfast, the trio drove from Tupelo to the Bynum Mounds. Margaret grew more tense with each passing mile, and was wound up tighter than a rubber band about to snap by the time they arrived at the entrance to the parking lot. It was still blocked off with police tape, and the officer on duty moved his cruiser and let them into the lot.

There were only a couple of parking spaces open, as the lot was almost full with official vehicles and what she assumed to be volunteers' automobiles. Two weeks into the search, there were still dozens of people searching for Sarah. Margaret took in the cars, the people, the church women giving out coffee, donuts, and bottles of water from their open trunk. She knew she should be grateful, but she felt only frustration. Why had Sarah not been found yet? Were these people actually looking for her, or just standing around socializing and eating free donuts? She reminded herself to breathe. As Rich pulled into a parking space, she felt the urge to jump out of the car, run across the grass, over the mounds, and scream for her daughter. It was everything she could do to maintain her composure. She sat in the front seat of Rich's old car, watching the volunteers talking near the mounds. She didn't move as Rich helped Grandma Ivy out of the backseat on the passenger side. After he closed the door, he opened Margaret's door and she stepped out, not taking her eyes off the mounds.

Rich placed his hand on Margaret's back. "Maggie, are you okay?"

Margaret nodded. At least, she thought she did.

Behind them, Grandma Ivy groaned. They both spun around.

Grandma Ivy was squinting at the field in front of the mounds, her brow knitted as if a migraine had come on.

"What is it?" Margaret asked.

"There's some, um, I guess you'd call it karma. Some bad karma here. Very bad."

"Grandma, what are you talking about?" Rich asked.

"A grudge. A painful past." She moaned again. "Karma must always be repaid."

"Grandma, you're scaring Maggie. Why don't you wait in the car while we go speak to the searchers and get an update?"

Grandma Ivy shook her head, not taking her eyes off the mounds.

Margaret nudged Rich out of the way and took a step toward the old woman.

"Grandma Ivy, what are you saying? What

karma? Do you know something about Sarah?"

Grandma Ivy looked at Margaret, and for a moment seemed to not remember who Margaret was. "No, I don't know anything about her specifically, but there is something very powerful in this place. No, not just powerful. Evil. There is bad karma at work here. Sarah isn't the first child to disappear from this place. I've known about them. Many of them. This has happened before."

"What are you talking about? How do you know this? Why didn't you say anything before?" Rich tried to step between his grandmother and Margaret.

Margaret stopped him. "No, Rich, let her talk. This is the first insight we've had about Sarah. Don't make her stop. Grandma Ivy, please continue."

"I haven't been out here in years, thirty-nine years to be exact, but the sight of this field suddenly brought back long forgotten memories. I remember coming here once as a child. My mother brought me and my sister out here for an afternoon picnic. The evening news had been talking about excavating the mounds and my mother loved archeology-type things. She had planned the picnic for two weeks.

"After we arrived, my grandmother came thundering into the gravel parking lot. It wasn't paved back then. She kicked up dust as she skidded to a stop in her old Packard. She stormed out of the car, screaming at my mother for bringing us here. I was confused by my grandmother's behavior. I had never heard her raise her voice before. I remember running to those woods over there and hiding behind a tree, thinking my grandmother had lost her mind. I could hear her screaming at my mother, something about the numerous stories of children who had disappeared near the mounds, telling my mother she was foolish for bringing us here. My mother fought back, telling my grandmother she sounded irrational, and yelling at her for frightening me. My sister remained on the picnic blanket, eating something, seemingly oblivious to the argument. But I was so shocked by it, I remained hidden in the trees."

"What else did your grandmother say?" Margaret asked.

She shrugged. "I don't remember anything else about the incident after that."

"So, she said other children had disappeared here before?" Margaret could hardly breathe.

"Yes, many have disappeared." Grandma Ivy stared at the mounds as if in a trance.

"Does the sheriff know this?" Rich asked.

"I don't know that he does, but I'll tell you it's been happening for two thousand years."

Margaret's face contorted in horror. "What?"

Grandma Ivy nodded.

Rich remained silent.

"How did they disappear?" Margaret asked.

"Same way as Sarah. Just vanished," Grandma Ivy mumbled.

"How did the parents get them back?"

"They didn't."

"What do you mean, they didn't?" Rich asked.

Grandma Ivy didn't answer.

"Grandma? They didn't come back?" Margaret said.

Grandma Ivy shook her head. "No, they didn't. They were taken...taken by the witches."

Chapter 12

The Search

Chiksa stoked the fire with a long stick, enjoying the sweet aroma of the venison roasting on the spit. He glanced up at women returning from the field, carrying baskets of maize on their heads. They smiled at him and he nodded. His people had seen an abundance of food this year, and he was immensely grateful to the gods for the bounty. The summer's weather had been perfect, the rainfall plentiful.

Not far behind the women, Chata was lumbering toward him, carrying a string of fish. By the size of his haul, it looked like Chata had a very good morning down at the river.

Chiksa was glad to see his brother, but the sadness on Chata's face sent pangs of guilt through Chiksa's chest. He was now caught in a web of deceit between his brother and his wife, between integrity and dishonesty. He could never tell Chata what Salina had done. He refused to even speak with Salina about it. He didn't want to know the sordid details. But as a leader who was to rule with honor, and as a brother who was responsible for his family, Chiksa's heart weighed heavy.

"Good morning, brother," Chata said. He set down the fish and rubbed his hands together, holding them up in front of the fire. "Smells good."

"Sure does. By the time this is finished cooking,

we'll all be hungry from the aroma. Looks like you had a nice catch this morning." Chiksa poked at the fire again, making sparks jump.

Chata nodded at the string of fish. "They were biting pretty good."

Chiksa kept his eyes on the fire. "How's your wife?"

"Mia's very sad."

Chiksa didn't know what to say next.

After a moment, Chata continued. "I don't understand how something like this could have happened. Mia's the kindest woman in the world. She doesn't deserve this. She said she fell asleep and when she awoke, only one of the twins was there. The other had vanished. There are no clues, no animal tracks, nothing to lead us to the whereabouts of the babe. I've asked everyone in the village, and no one saw or heard anything."

Chiksa wanted to console his brother's grief, but couldn't find the words—words that would be lies. He kept poking the fire.

"How is Salina?" Chata asked.

"She's better. I'm very relieved I didn't lose her."

"You are lucky, brother."

"Yes, I am." Chiksa glanced at his brother, who was staring at the fire. Chata's eyes were drawn, with dark circles beneath. Losing their father had been tough on Chata, and he'd been so concerned about losing Mia during childbirth, but instead he'd lost one of his babes. Not by illness or accident, but by a promise that could not be broken. A promise to an old woman who offered magic. If Chata knew what had happened, he would kill Chiksa right here, right now, with his bare hands. Chiksa couldn't say he'd blame him. Maybe Chiksa deserved such a death for his cowardly silence. Maybe he should have killed the old woman instead of letting her destroy his family, but he didn't know if that would've been any better. If he'd attacked the old woman, she might have killed Salina.

What was he supposed to do now? Maybe he should tell Chata the truth. If Chiksa was any kind of man, he would be forthcoming with his brother. But what would happen to Salina then? He'd gone through all of this to avoid losing her. If word got out about what she did and his secrecy about it, his reign as the tribal chief would end swiftly. If by some miracle his people blamed Salina and not him, he didn't think he would be able to save her from the wrath the tribe would surely carry out.

Chata picked up his fish and turned to walk away. "I'll see you later, brother. I need to go check on my wife."

"Chata?"

Chata turned.

"I…um…need to…please tell her I'm very sorry for what happened."

Chata nodded and continued on.

***

After scaling the fish, Chata went home and found his wife sitting in darkness in their hut, rocking their infant, tears streaming down her face. She dried her cheeks with the palm of her hand when he entered.

"Are you all right?" he asked.

She nodded.

"Then why do you cry?"

She looked at him, obviously wanting to say something, but hesitated.

"Tell me," he urged as he pulled up a chair.

"I heard something."

"What? What did you hear?"

"One of the young girls from the village saw me outside getting water and she stopped to talk. She said something strange."

"Strange?"

She nodded. "About Salina."

"What about her?"

"She said she thought Salina's baby had died."

Chata shrugged. "Everyone knows her baby died. Why would anyone ask about that?"

The babe in Mia's arms fussed at her breast and she looked down for a moment.

Chata waited for her to reposition the infant.

She looked back at Chata, but remained silent.

"What is it, Mia? What did she say about Salina's baby?"

"She said she saw Salina carrying something cradled in her arms like one holds an infant."

Chata's face paled. "When was this?"

Mia shook her head. "She didn't know exactly. She knew it was in the last few nights. She said she heard Salina's baby died at least a full moon ago, so she must have heard wrong because she was sure Salina was cradling a baby. She wondered how she could have been so mistaken when Salina's baby was indeed alive. I asked her if she saw a baby. She thought about it for a moment and said she didn't actually see what Salina was carrying, only that she was carrying something cradled in her arms."

Chata stood. "Why didn't she stop her?"

"Chata, she didn't know for sure what Salina was carrying. Still doesn't. And she's almost a child herself. She'd have no right to stop the wife of the chief and certainly no right to question her."

Chata stomped toward the door.

"Where are you going?"

"I'm going to talk to my brother. I'm going to find out what happened that night."

"Chata, it can't be true. If Salina has our baby, then where is it? She doesn't have a baby hiding in her hut. Someone would have heard it. And why would she do such a thing?"

"I don't know. I don't understand any of this, and I certainly wouldn't believe my own brother would hide something like that from me, although I sensed something strange when I spoke with him earlier today. I'm not sure what I'm going to say, but I need to speak with Chiksa." He reached the door and turned back around. "If our child has been taken, I promise you I will get to the bottom of this and I will get her back. I will kill to get her back."

Chapter 13

History

Margaret didn't sleep very well that night. She tossed and turned, dozing for only an hour or so at a time, kicking the quilt off and getting chilled, pulling it back on and sweating, over and over again. She stared at the darkened picture of the children and the angel, Grandma Ivy's story playing in her head. Was the woman growing senile? Or had there really been children taken from the mounds before? And if so, did the sheriff know anything about them? She couldn't even fathom witches. They were imaginary, weren't they? Grandma Ivy seemed so serious, and Margaret had never doubted anything the woman said before.

Margaret looked at the bedside clock for the fifth time—3:35 a.m. There would be no sleep tonight. She might as well get up and get dressed. As soon as Rich woke up, she'd be ready to go back to the mounds. Maybe today would be the day they found something. She doubted it would have anything to do with witches, though.

As she towel-dried her hair after a quick shower, she thought she heard someone in the kitchen. She hoped she hadn't woken anyone, but maybe everyone else was having trouble sleeping, too. She cracked open the bathroom door and looked down the hallway toward the kitchen. There were no lights on, only the sapphire glow of a computer screen illuminating the hallway.

She padded into the kitchen and found Rich sitting at the table with his laptop.

"Hey, you can't sleep, either?" she asked.

He jumped.

"I'm sorry. I didn't mean to startle you."

"That's okay. I didn't hear you. Having trouble sleeping?"

She nodded and grabbed a glass from the cabinet. She opened the refrigerator, flooding the room with white light. "Grandma's witch story has me wondering if something bigger is going on here. How is it possible that there are zero clues about Sarah's whereabouts? I don't believe in witches, but right now I can't figure out if I'm just grasping at straws or if it's actually beginning to make sense. I just wish we could find Sarah." She knew the thoughts coming out of her mouth were as jumbled as they were in her head.

Rich rose from the table and reached for her hand.

She set the jug of juice and the glass down on the table and took his hand.

He pulled her into his arms.

She allowed him to hold her. How did he know the best thing to do for her at this moment was to hold her? Her own husband wouldn't have done that. Where was her little girl? Was Sarah suffering? Was she dead? Margaret's tears began to flow. She was so tired of crying, but she couldn't stop them.

Rich held her tightly and stroked her damp hair as she cried.

When her sobs finally slowed, she looked into his eyes. "I'm sorry. I didn't mean to fall apart on you."

"There's no reason to be sorry. I don't know

what I'd do in your position. You think you're Wonder Woman, but I know better. You're still the little Maggie I've known my whole life, and I'm here for you. I hope you know that."

She looked off to the side, thinking she should break the emotional connection growing between them. It wasn't appropriate. But she didn't let go of him. She didn't want to. His warmth was comforting. She couldn't remember the last time Thomas had held her. "I'm certainly not Wonder Woman. I think I used to be, but something happened along the way. I'm just, well, I'm just a mess now. You couldn't possibly understand."

He placed his finger under her chin and tilted her face up. "I understand you very well."

She looked into his brown eyes, and the two of them remained still. His touch and his gaze exuded caring and kindness. There was no anger, no judgment, no years of emotional baggage and pent-up aggravation. Thomas used to look at her this way. Now his looks were full of frustration and sometimes pity. This man, this longtime friend—his gaze was one of acceptance and even love. He leaned forward and kissed her gently on the lips. She gave into his kiss, desiring a deeper, more passionate connection. She wrapped her fingers into his curly hair and pulled him closer. Abruptly, she pulled away. "I'm sorry, Rich. I can't."

He let her go. "No, no, it's my fault. I'm sorry. I don't know what came over me."

He sat back down at his computer as she poured juice into the glass. An uncomfortable silence surrounded them. She put the jug back into the refrigerator and paused at the door after it closed. She needed Rich's help to find Sarah. She couldn't allow this moment to ruin their friendship. She pulled out a chair next to him.

"I'm sorry, Rich. I don't want it to be awkward between us."

"No. I shouldn't have done that."

"It's okay. I was having a moment. I let it happen."

"I don't want you to think I'm trying to take advantage of you. I'd never do that."

"And I know you well enough to know that you would never do that. Let's just forget it."

He nodded.

"So, what are you doing?" she asked, looking at his computer screen.

"I'm searching for anything relating to Grandma's story. The *Journal* has been in business a long, long time, and if a child was missing from Bynum Mounds, I'd think it would have been reported."

"Well, forget that she said they were taken by witches. I don't even understand that comment. What year would she be talking about, being there as a child? I don't even know how old Grandma Ivy is." She took a sip of the juice.

"I'm not exactly sure. I'm looking back as far as I can. She mentioned her grandmother's Packard, and those were made between 1899 and 1958, so that narrows it down."

He picked up his notebook. There was a lot of scribbling on it, mostly years, numbers, calculations. Margaret couldn't make any of it out in the dim light.

"I found one missing back in 1978."

"So, she was right? There were other children?"

He nodded. "But this one was a boy, and that was about forty years ago. That wouldn't be far enough back."

"Did you find any more?"

"Yeah, I found a girl missing in 1943."

"Really?" Margaret did the math in her head. "Maybe that's the one she was referring to, or maybe that was just after she was there. So, her grandmother would have been fifty at the time? And knew of children who disappeared before that? Maybe her grandmother was talking about 1910 or 1920? Did you find anything from that time period?"

"That's exactly how I figured it, too, but I didn't find anything from before 1943. But both the girl from 1943 and the boy from 1978 were reported missing from the same area. I think that's something to go on."

Margaret rubbed the muscles in her aching neck and calculated the years in her head. "It couldn't possibly be the same abductor as now, though. If he was, say, twenty in 1943, that would make him, what, ninety-five now? No one that age could just disappear with all those people searching out there."

"True. So, how did they disappear? I've been searching for hours, but there are no other stories about them or what may have happened to them. I'm going to call Sheriff Miller as soon as it gets light outside. He may be able to find out more information."

He stared at the computer screen, but Margaret could tell he wasn't really looking at it.

"What? What are you thinking, Rich?"

"There's something else." He didn't look at her.

"What?" She was frightened by his demeanor.

"The boy in '78 and the girl in '43…" He turned to her. "As far as I can tell, they were never found."

"Never found?"

He shook his head.

She stared at him.

He didn't break eye contact.

She felt the heat of fear rise up the back of her neck. Her hands clenched into fists and started trembling. The room felt like it was closing in around her.

There was more. She could read it on his face.

"What is it, Rich? What else?"

He opened his mouth to say something and closed it again.

"Rich, what else?"

"They were both twins."

Chapter 14

Destruction

Chiksa looked up as his brother approached, and was about to ask if Chata had forgotten something when Chata punched him hard across the jaw. Chiksa didn't fall, but he was forced back a step and dropped his fire stick. He rubbed his jaw as he looked at his brother. That was no brotherly jab; that was an all-out assault. Chata's eyes were wild with anger, his face red.

"Chata, are you crazy? What was that for?"

"Why don't you tell me? Tell me where my daughter is."

"I don't know what you're talking about. How would I know?"

Chata lowered his voice and got right in Chiksa's face. He was trembling with rage. "Look me in the eyes and tell me you don't know what happened to my daughter."

Chiksa couldn't say anything.

"Tell me, Chiksa!" Chata shoved him in the chest.

"I can't tell you anything," Chiksa said, still rubbing his aching jaw. "I don't know anything."

"A child doesn't just disappear from a hut in the middle of the night. You know something. I know you do."

Chiksa turned away and bent over to pick up his fire stick. "I've never lied to you. I don't know where your child is." He poked the fire.

"Look at me and say that." The wind had shifted and the smoke from the fire surrounded them. Chiksa kept his eyes on the fire. "Chata, I don't know anything."

"I can tell when you're not being truthful. You know something. Tell me."

Chiksa didn't answer.

"Is it Salina?"

Chiksa's shoulders tensed.

"Did Salina take my daughter?"

Chiksa didn't answer, but the muscle in his jaw twitched. He took his eyes off the fire and stared at the forest behind it.

"Answer me, Chiksa. What happened?"

Chiksa exhaled and looked back at the fire. "I don't know. I don't know what happened."

"Do you have my daughter?"

"No!" He turned toward Chata. "No, of course I don't." His heart pounded as he tried to conceive a way around this. He had never lied to his brother before. Maybe he should tell him the truth. They were warriors. Surely together they'd be able to find this old woman and get the child back.

The look on Chata's face made him decided to tell the truth and to face his brother's wrath. "You know Salina almost died in childbirth."

"I know that."

"I went out to the clearing where Father is buried and I prayed to him for help."

Chata waited for Chiksa to continue.

"An old woman appeared from the woods."

"What woman? Someone from our village?"

Chiksa shook his head. "I've never seen her

before, but she knew everything about me. She called Salina by name and said Salina was on the brink of death. She told me to bring Salina to the clearing and she would make her whole again. She would heal her. Chata, you have to understand, Salina was going to die." He looked at Chata, begging him to understand. "Whatever this woman wanted, I would give her to keep my wife alive."

"Wait, wait, wait. She wanted my daughter?"

"No, I didn't know the price she wanted. She only whispered it to Salina. I was there, but I didn't hear what was said. Salina agreed to whatever the old woman asked for, and the old woman gave her a potion. The next day, Salina was better."

"What does this have to do with my daughter?"

Chiksa hesitated. "I think the old woman told Salina she wanted a child. Salina was terrified the next day and said she couldn't pay the woman what she had promised. I told her we couldn't go back on our promise. I was afraid the woman would come back and kill Salina. I didn't know what the debt was at the time. I'm still not sure, but I have a suspicion. I haven't spoken with Salina about it, but I told her she could not go back on the debt. She must pay the woman's price."

Chata stared at Chiksa. He didn't respond.

"Why do you think your daughter's disappearance has anything to do with Salina?" Chiksa asked.

"Because someone saw her," Chata spat.

"Who? We asked everyone."

"One of the village girls. She didn't realize what she had seen at the time, but she has come forward. She saw Salina cradling something the same time my daughter disappeared."

"Is she sure that's what she saw?"

"My daughter is gone! She didn't walk away on her own. Chiksa, if you know what happened, be a man and tell me."

"I'm sorry, brother. I've told you all I know."

Chata didn't move for a moment, then he rushed Chiksa and tackled him, delivering a harsh blow to Chiksa's stomach. Chiksa wasn't completely caught off guard, suspecting Chata was ready for a fight, but he hadn't been prepared for the brutal strength of his brother's attack. Chiksa had always been the stronger of the two, but Chata was now overflowing with anger and adrenaline. He was on top of Chiksa, punching him in the face. Chiksa tried to ward off the blows. He bucked his hips and sent Chata flying.

"Chata! Stop this! This isn't going to solve anything."

"You have taken my baby from my hut in the middle of the night. You have given my child to some old woman whom you don't even know. And you want me to stop?!"

Chiksa climbed to his feet. He backed around the fire, his hands in front of him. "Chata!"

"I will not stop until you are dead!"

Chata darted around the fire, tackled Chiksa again, and the two fell to the ground. Chiksa's head was dangerously close to the fire, but what worried him more was the large stone Chata was now holding over his head.

"I will bash your head in. I will kill you for what you've done. Then I will go after your wife."

"Chata! Stop!" Mia screamed from behind him.

In the moment of surprise, Chiksa threw Chata off. Chiksa quickly rose to his feet, wiping the blood from his lip. As he backed around the fire, he saw Salina at a distance, hidden in the brush.

Chata looked at his wife. "It's true, Mia. What you heard is true."

Mia, clutching her infant, looked at Chiksa, her eyes dark. "You took my child?" she asked softly.

Chiksa shook his head.

***

Salina was horrified to see the brothers fighting, but when she heard what Mia said, it all made sense. They knew.

She turned and ran through the woods. If she stayed, two things would happen: her husband would lose his village and his family, and the tribe would put her to death. The thought of her own death wasn't bad. Maybe she deserved it for what she had done. But she couldn't allow her husband to be disgraced in front of his people.

She should go back to her hut and get her things. No. That wasn't an option. She had to leave now. She wished she could undo everything she had done, but she didn't know how. Maybe she should go to the clearing and see if she could find the old woman, but the brothers would head there, too.

She ran for what seemed like hours, branches scratching her face, vines and barbs scraping her legs. Finally, she stopped at the base of a large cedar tree to rest and think. She wondered what good it had been to get her life back only to lose it again. Everything she knew, everyone she knew, was now gone, taken away in an instant. She wished Chiksa would have let her die with her baby. Sobs escaped her throat as she sat alone in the dark forest, wondering what to do next.

Chapter 15

Myrtle Brooks

Margaret and Rich were still sitting at the kitchen table as the sun rose.

"Will you take me back out to the mounds?" Margaret asked.

"Of course. Do you want to go right now?"

"Do you think Grandma Ivy would be up to going back? I would like to know what else she remembers. Maybe we should wait for her to get up."

Rich looked concerned. His grandmother was in good health but she was old. He didn't know how much excitement she could take.

"Of course, I'll go back out there with you, dear," Grandma Ivy said as she entered the kitchen, dressed and ready to start her day. She took a cup from the dish strainer next to the sink and headed toward the coffee pot, but the coffee hadn't been made. As she made some, she said, "Margaret, I knew you'd want to go back to the mounds today, and I hope you don't mind but I've invited an old friend to join us."

"What friend?" Rich asked. His grandmother had always been a loner. He didn't know she had any friends.

"My oldest and dearest friend, Myrtle. Myrtle Brooks. I'm not sure you'd remember her. You might. She hasn't come around for many years, but she has a sense of these things. I don't know if you'd call her psychic, but she certainly knows things."

Margaret sat up straight. "Do you think she knows anything about what you said yesterday? About missing children?"

Grandma Ivy stared at the coffee pot as if looking at it would make it brew faster. "My dear, if anyone knows what's happening at the Bynum Mounds, it's Myrtle." Grandma Ivy glanced up at the clock above the sink—6:00 AM. "She said she'd be here at first light. If I know her, she'll be knocking on the door shortly."

"Well, I guess I'd better get dressed, then." Rich rose. "I'll be ready in ten. Maggie, why don't you fill Grandma Ivy in on what we found online?"

***

When Margaret heard the screen door slam, she knew Grandma Ivy's friend had arrived. She ran to her room and slipped on her sneakers. As she exited, she glanced in the mirror, grimaced, and smoothed down her hair. She grabbed a rubber band off the nightstand and braided her hair down the right side. She wished she had more fashion sense, but today, a red rubber band would have to do.

She left the bedroom and heard voices near the front door.

As she approached, she saw Grandma Ivy speaking with a short elderly woman. This woman was not the grandmotherly type Ivy was. She seemed quite bold with her blue jeans, hot pink blouse, her powder white hair, and a flowered scarf wrapped around her neck. She spun toward Margaret when Margaret approached.

Grandma Ivy smiled and said, "Margaret, this is

my dear friend, Myrtle Brooks."

Margaret offered her hand to Myrtle, but Myrtle didn't move. She stared at Margaret as if she was seeing a ghost. Her jaw hung open.

"Hello, Ms. Brooks. It's a pleasure to meet you." Margaret awkwardly pulled her hand back.

Myrtle still didn't move.

"Myrtle." Grandma Ivy touched her arm.

Rich came in from outside. "The car is ready to go." He stopped in midstride, seeing all three women staring at each other in silence.

Myrtle seemed to come out of her haze. "Yes, we should go." She nodded, but didn't take her eyes off Margaret.

Grandma Ivy took Myrtle's arm and turned her toward the door.

As the older women walked down the porch steps arm in arm, Rich approached Margaret. "What was that all about?"

"I have no idea."

"She seems like she knows you."

"I've never seen her before in my life."

"Well, I've never seen her before, either."

"Really? I thought your grandmother said you would remember her."

"Nope. Never seen her before this moment."

"That's strange," Margaret said as she grabbed her purse off the table near the front door.

Rich held open the door. "I think it's going to be an interesting day."

***

By the time the group reached the mounds, the

sun was firmly on its morning arc, and there were at least a dozen people milling around the parking lot. Not nearly as many as the day before, but it was Monday and people needed to go back to work. Margaret wondered if Emily was on her way to school. She would call the house later and speak with her mother-in-law. She was still in no mood to speak with Thomas.

As she climbed out of the car, a few people glanced at her sadly but most ignored her, not realizing who she was. She suddenly had the feeling these people were probably tourists, not searchers, but the police tape was still in place and the police cruiser was still guarding the entrance. They would soon forget about Sarah. They would go back to their comfortable lives where their families were together. Margaret didn't know what she would do when that time came, and she was terrified it was coming soon. They were approaching three weeks since Sarah had disappeared. No child could survive in the woods alone for that amount of time. Margaret couldn't even imagine going back to her house, her life, her husband, without Sarah. But she would have to. Emily was there. Emily needed her.

"Her presence is very strong here," Myrtle said as she climbed from the back seat.

Margaret spun toward her. "Sarah's?"

Myrtle hesitated before she spoke. "Yes, Sarah is here, too."

"What do you mean, 'too'? Someone else is here besides Sarah?"

Myrtle nodded and walked toward the grass. "There are many here. Too many."

Behind her, Margaret heard Grandma Ivy say, "Let them go. Myrtle knows a lot about this place. She can teach Margaret many things. If anyone can bring back Margaret's daughter, it's Myrtle. Let them go."

Myrtle walked toward the mounds, across the grass that was in dire need of cutting since the maintenance crew hadn't been allowed into the area since the disappearance.

Margaret followed closely, waiting for the woman's next words.

"It's been many years since I've been here."

Margaret remained quiet.

"Thirty-nine years, to be exact."

"That's the same thing Grandma Ivy said. Why thirty-nine, and how do you remember the exact time?"

"Oh, I remember it well. It's not something I could forget. Someday I'll tell you the whole story."

Margaret didn't know what to think about Myrtle. Her mannerisms were a bit odd. The words coming out of her mouth were downright strange. But if Grandma Ivy said Myrtle could help, then Margaret would listen to her.

When they reached the far side of the lawn, Myrtle stopped and turned to Margaret. She began removing the flowered scarf from her neck. "What do you know about this place?"

"Nothing about the Bynum Mounds, only the story of Witch Dance."

She dabbed her forehead with her scarf. "You need to learn about the Native people. Learn the legend, the history."

"Why? How will that help get my daughter back?"

"If I tell you, you won't believe me. You need to learn about the history of this place on your own. Once you know it, then you will believe what I have to say. Then and only then will we have a chance to bring your child back."

"Back? Back from where? Does someone have her?"

"Yes, someone has her." She looked toward the mounds. "Someone certainly has her, but not here."

"Not here? Then where?"

"I can't tell you where, but I can tell you one important thing. You will need every shred of strength and courage you can muster, plus more, to get your daughter back."

Margaret gaped at Myrtle. "We need to tell the sheriff."

"No, the sheriff can't help you. You need your own strength."

"I don't feel very strong, just confused."

"Your confusion will go away as you learn. And you will be strong when the time comes. You will need all the fortitude you possess to get her back."

"Get her back from where?"

Myrtle grunted. "You need to learn the history."

Margaret looked at the mounds. None of this made any sense. Is it possible these women were simply having the same senile delusion? Is it possible they were telling the truth? She looked back at Myrtle. "Is Sarah alive? Is it possible to get her back?"

Myrtle grinned. "Yes, yes, she's alive." The smile faded from her lips. "I don't know if it's possible."

Myrtle turned and began walking back toward the parking lot, her scarf dragging the ground behind her.

Margaret followed closely, trying to not step on the scarf. "What do you mean, you don't know if it's possible?"

When Myrtle stopped and turned back to Margaret, Margaret had to stop abruptly to keep from bumping into her.

Myrtle narrowed her eyes at Margaret.

"What is it?" Margaret asked.

"You look just like her, you know."

"Just like who?"

"Someone I knew a long, long time ago." Myrtle squinted as if studying Margaret's face. Her expression softened to one of...love?

"Who?"

"Her name was Mia."

Lori Crane

Chapter 16

Salina's Rescue

Salina wrapped her arms around her knees as she sat on the cold, damp forest floor, rocking and sobbing. The tree frogs were croaking at an ear-piercing volume. Their song announced a coming storm, and thunder rumbled in the distance. Was there shelter near here? She looked around, not knowing where she was. She had never been to this part of the forest. She thought about what she had done, about the woman who had caused this, about her husband who had now lost his father, his child, and his wife. How did this happen? How did her life so quickly go from happiness to near death to promise to complete ruin? Her child had died. Yes, she'd wanted to die after that, but deep down, she'd known death would solve nothing. It would've been a coward's way out. As she grew closer to death, she'd begun to realize she didn't want to give up on life, on Chiksa, on the possibility of growing a family. Dying of sadness was not the future she had planned. Since she was a young girl, her plan had been to marry a good man and raise many strong babies. She'd momentarily lost sight of that plan, and by the time she realized it was happening, death had already taken a grip on her body. The closer death came, the more she'd feared it. The old woman had come along at the right time. Days before she appeared, Salina would have denied the chance to live. Days later, Salina would have already been dead. Oma had perfect timing.

But the woman's price had been too much. What would've been a fair price for life? Salina didn't know. On her deathbed, she'd been afraid and would have agreed to anything. Not that it was an excuse for what she did later, but she hadn't been thinking clearly at the time. She never considered the repercussions. Now it was too late, and she couldn't return to her tribe. She couldn't get the child back and return it to Mia. Would the old woman really have killed Salina if Salina hadn't paid the price? Yes, Salina was certain she would have. She knew the woman had the power to do so.

It seemed depressing and exhausting, but Salina had no choice. She must leave her village and begin a new life. She must do it for Chiksa. Chiksa's strongest trait was his pride. He was proud of his lineage, of the way his grandfather and his father had led their people. He'd dreamed of nothing his entire life except to follow in their footsteps. It would destroy him to be shamed in front of his own people. She couldn't allow that to happen.

She also couldn't let this come between Chiksa and his brother. They were all the village had left, and they had to remain united for the sake of the people. If the village had to find out what had happened, she wanted them to believe it was her doing and hers alone. They would call upon the elders for direction, and if the elders suspected she was alive, they would hunt her down and exact their punishment. She would not give them the opportunity. She would vanish. Because she was the chief's wife, the elders might decide to let her go with the hopes she never returned to the village. In their eyes she would cease to exist. Eventually, Chiksa would remarry and have an heir.

Salina cried. It would not be her child who'd lead the tribe in the future. It would be someone she didn't know, someone who never knew her. She would just be a story in the village legends, a small blemish that meant nothing. She would become a lesson to be learned, a story for elders to pass down to children, an example of evil and consequences.

She stopped crying and lay down on the hard ground, curling into a ball, wishing for death to take her now. The frogs croaked louder as rain tapped the tops of the trees. Soon it covered her completely in a blanket of showers. Thunder boomed, and the raindrops mixed with her tears.

***

The morning sun speckled her face through the empty branches of the fall trees. She didn't mean to fall to sleep, but apparently, she had. She sat up, wet from the night's rainstorm. Her neck was stiff. Sleeping on the hard ground had played havoc on her back and shoulders. She stretched and moaned, and then realized she should be quiet. What if they were searching for her? She must keep moving, get as far away from the village as possible.

As quickly as she could, she rose and moved deeper into the forest, not sure where she was headed, but following the same direction she had last night. How far must she walk to be safe? How far must she travel until no one knew who she was, where she had come from, or what she had done?

As the sun reached its peak, she crossed a small stream and knelt down to drink and wash her face.

When she saw her reflection in the stream, she began to cry again. What looked back at her was a haggard and muddy woman, with unkempt hair, puffy eyes, and deep sadness. She looked like death.

"Can I help you, my dear?" a woman's voice said from the other side of the creek.

Salina jumped and backed up to the nearest tree.

"Don't run, Salina. I saved your life. I certainly wouldn't let you die now."

Salina froze. It was the old woman. Salina didn't remember the woman's features, but she did remember the black cloak. And she remembered the voice, the way the woman drew out the *ee* sound in *Salina* was almost mesmerizing, like the hiss of a snake. You knew you should move away from it, but there was something captivating about the way that forked tongue darted in and out.

"Do you need some help? Why are you so far from home?"

Salina didn't answer.

"Well?"

Salina realized if she could be truthful with anyone, it was this woman. After all, this woman started this entire chain of events. "Where's the baby?"

"Oh, she's being well cared for. Thank you for bringing her to me so quickly."

Salina almost said, "You're welcome," but thought better of it and remained silent.

"So, you didn't answer me. Why are you so far from home?"

"I no longer have a home. They found out what I did—what I did for you—and I've run away before they kill me."

The woman shook her head. "No, no. What you did was pay a debt. It wasn't for me. It was a price you voluntarily paid. And don't worry, I wouldn't let them kill you. I spent a lot of time on that potion to keep you alive."

"I don't think you could stop them. They're probably looking for me right now."

"Honestly, I wouldn't need to stop them. They couldn't kill you, even if they tried. The potion you drank not only gave you life but eternal life."

Salina gawked at the woman. "That's not possible."

"Don't believe me?"

Salina shook her head.

"Well, let's try this." She reached down, no more than a foot from where she was standing, and grabbed a copperhead by the neck. The woman tossed it at Salina, who tried to swat it away. One hand glanced close to the snake's head but missed, while the other grabbed the tail. The snake spun around and bit her on the arm. Salina dropped it and it slithered away into the brush. She looked up at the old woman in terror.

"Oh, don't be afraid. There is nothing and no one that can harm you."

Salina was afraid to move. The poison would quickly make its way up her arm and into her body. She would be dead soon.

"I can see you don't believe me. Let's sit down and wait for you to die." The old woman sat on a stump while Salina remained standing. "How long do you think we should wait?"

Salina didn't answer.

"I say let's wait until the sun passes that tree right there." She pointed up to a branch.

Salina shuddered as she tried to breathe. Shouldn't she start to feel something? After a few minutes, she rubbed the area where the snake had bitten her. No blood, no swelling, no fang marks. She looked at the woman.

The woman smiled. "Yes, it bit you. I've done no magic. You are immortal."

Salina looked back down at her arm. Still nothing.

"Now do you believe me?"

"What was in the potion that would do something like this?"

The woman rose from the stump, pushing the hood of her cloak from her head. She wasn't old like Salina remembered. She was young and beautiful. "The ingredients of the potion are my secret. Maybe someday I will tell you." The woman started to walk away but stopped and turned. "You might as well come with me since you don't have anywhere else to go."

Salina didn't want to go with her, but the woman was right.

"Come, dear. I'll show you things you've never seen before, take you to places you've never been. You'll enjoy it. You'll see." The woman walked into the forest.

Salina followed.

Chapter 17

Missing Children

After a strange and perplexing day with Myrtle at the Bynum Mounds, Margaret was exhausted, physically and mentally. She climbed into the front seat of Rich's car and rested her head on the side window, wishing she could just go to sleep and wake up with this nightmare over. Another day had passed with no sign of Sarah and no leads. It was a day filled with weird stories from two old women who most likely were suffering from some sort of collective dementia, but Margaret forced herself to hold on to the possibility that the women knew something she was not able to understand. Karma? Witches? And who's Mia? Margaret wanted to look into the back seat and ask the ladies questions, but she didn't feel like she could process anymore information right now. She felt as if she was slipping down into some rabbit hole. The only thing keeping her from screaming was Myrtle saying Sarah was alive. With that remote possibility, Margaret would wade through this absurdity to find her.

"Maggie?" Rich said as he put the car into reverse.

"Hmm," she responded, too tired to open her eyes, listening to the tires whistle as he backed out of the parking space.

"Sheriff Miller called my cell while you were at the mounds with Myrtle."

Margaret was suddenly very much awake. "Did he say anything about Sarah?"

Rich shook his head. "He said he thinks I'm on to something with researching the other missing children. He said he will be waiting for us at the house when we get back."

Margaret watched him turn onto the main road, wished the car would go faster.

When they arrived, the sun had just set behind the house, the sky fading from pink to indigo. As they turned into the driveway, the old Lincoln's headlights shone across the sheriff leaning on the trunk of his squad car, chewing on a long piece of grass. He watched them pull up into the front yard to not block his car.

"Sheriff," Margaret said as she exited the car before Rich had even put it in park. "Do you have any word on Sarah?"

"Why don't we go inside and sit down." He tossed the piece of grass on the ground and headed toward the door, not waiting for anyone to show him the way.

Once they were seated at the kitchen table, Grandma Ivy offered them drinks and started making supper. "Sheriff, you're welcome to stay, if you'd like."

"Thank you for the offer, Ms. Ivy, but I'll only be here a little bit. I have a lot of work to do at the office."

Margaret fidgeted with the edge of a paper napkin left on the table from that morning. She was about to jump over the table and demand he start talking.

Sheriff Miller directed his comments at Rich. "So, I looked into the two missing children you mentioned."

"And?" Margaret said.

The sheriff looked at her and his face softened. "Mrs. Speedwell, I'm afraid they were never found. The files are still marked as unsolved. They're so old, I didn't even know they were back there in the old records." He looked back at Rich. "I did find something, though. I found another missing child."

"What?" Margaret asked.

"When?" asked Rich.

"Eighteen sixty-one." He pulled out a copy of a newspaper article and placed it on the table. "The *Natchez Gazette* reported a child missing from the area. As far as I can tell, that child wasn't found, either, but with the war starting right on the heels of the report, I'm afraid I couldn't find anything else written about the child. The paper shut down during the war, and we don't have police records going back that far."

"That's three," Margaret said to Rich.

"I think there's actually four," the sheriff said. "I spoke with a descendant of the man who owned the paper back then, and he told me his great-great-grandfather left records of all the *Gazette*'s stories in the attic of their old family home. The man still lives in the house. So, we snooped around up there for hours looking for the record of the missing child report in 1861.

"Fortunately, the grandfather kept well-organized archives, and we eventually found his record of the story. There were no reporter's notes, just a copy of the article itself. On it was something handwritten at the bottom of the page. Between the bad handwriting and the fading ink, we think it said, and I quote"—he pulled a piece of paper out of his breast pocket and read— "'Is this like the child who disappeared in 1837 that my grandfather told me about?'" We couldn't tell if it is the great-great-grandfather's handwriting, and we couldn't find any other records of missing children."

They sat in stunned silence.

"So, Rich, I was thinking maybe you could look into a missing child in 1837. I bet you have more sources to turn to than I do. I really don't know where to look next when it comes to publishing."

Rich looked down at the article in his hands.

"What does any of this have to do with Sarah?" Margaret said. "I've listened to you all talk about karma, missing children, legends, newspapers, witches, but my daughter is still out there in the woods!" She stood up. "She's six years old and she's out there alone in the woods!"

Rich tried to rub her arm. "We'll find her, Maggie, we'll find her."

She yanked her arm away. She didn't need comfort right now. She needed answers. "She's been gone almost three weeks!"

The sheriff grimaced.

Margaret ran out of the room.

The sheriff looked at Rich. "I'm sorry I upset her."

"It's okay. It's been a long day."

The sheriff rose. "Well, there's nothing else for now, so I guess I'll be going." He paused. "Did she say if her other daughter is speaking yet?"

"She hasn't said anything to me about it. I don't know that she's spoken with her husband yesterday or today. I'll tell her to call you."

"Okay." He nodded at Ivy and Myrtle. "Good night, ladies."

"I'll walk you out," Rich said, and followed the sheriff out of the room.

***

Margaret washed her face in the bathroom and looked in the mirror. "I'm coming apart at the seams," she whispered to herself. She dried her face on the white towel that smelled like bleach. She looked back into the mirror and sighed. "Pull it together, Margaret. You're going to be no good to anyone if you don't pull it together. Ending up in the nuthouse isn't going to help."

She decided to return to the kitchen and apologize to everyone for her outburst. She took a step into the hallway and was surprised she didn't hear voices coming from the kitchen. She wondered if they had gone outside. She stopped to listen for them and heard Myrtle and Ivy in the kitchen whispering to each other. Why were they whispering?

"How long do you think can you keep this a secret?" Myrtle asked.

"Shhh. This is neither the time nor the place to talk about this."

"It's going to come to light whether you want it to or not, and you know as well as I do that we cannot save this little girl without digging up the past."

There was a pause. Margaret heard a spoon being tapped on the side of a pot and assumed Ivy was standing at the stove stirring something.

Myrtle continued. "You need to prepare yourself, Ivy. He's going to find out the truth."

Lori Crane

Chapter 18

Oma

"You can stay here with me…with us," Oma said to Salina as they entered the coolness of the cave.

Salina didn't see anyone else, so she didn't know who the woman was referring to as *us*. There were no burning torches, no smoke, no flame, but the cave was strangely well lit. She thought the sun must be shining through a hole somewhere, but they had just walked for miles and the sun was starting to set. It was not the source of this brightness. There was a firepit in the corner, but it wasn't lit. There were some cots on the damp floor and a table in the center, surrounded by chairs. Someone had gone to a lot of trouble to make the place habitable, but it was still a cave. It smelled musty and the walls looked damp. Salina imagined bats coming out at night.

A sound came from the dark path on the right. Drip, drip, drip. She wondered if the drips were coming from the walls, or if there was a freshwater source down the path. If there was water, there were probably lizards, too. She hated lizards. "Who is *us*?" she asked.

"Oh, there are a few of us here." Oma approached the firepit, carrying a pot. She waved her hand over the pit and a fire came to life with a whooshing sound.

Salina's jaw fell open.

Oma placed the pot on the flames. "Would you

care for something warm to drink?"

It had been nearly two days since Salina ate anything. The only thing she'd drunk was a sip from the stream just before Oma had appeared. Salina didn't want to become comfortable here, but her body disagreed with her mind. "Yes," she said softly.

Within a few minutes, Oma handed her a carved bowl filled with steaming liquid.

Salina drank deeply. The heat burned her throat, but it felt good.

"Now," Oma said, "You are welcome to stay. You're really one of us now anyway. You'll learn to like it, you'll see."

"What will the price be for that?" she said.

"No need to worry about that now."

Salina took another sip of the warm liquid and sat down on one of the cots.

She didn't remember going to sleep, but woke hours later and found herself lying on the same cot, covered with a bearskin. The fire roared as if someone had just stoked it, but then she remembered Oma had started it with a wave of her hand. She imagined no one would need to stoke such a fire. She sat up and looked at it. There was no wood in the pit, only stone. The flames glowed a golden amber, with no smoke rising from it. There was no ash, no popping sounds of wood burning. The flames were almost like yellow water, except they were flowing upward.

"I thought the same the first time I saw that, too," a voice said from the other side of the room.

Salina looked in the direction of the voice but could see only a dark shadow. "Who are you?"

"I live here with Oma."

"Do you have a name?"

"Yes, but you don't need to know it."

The girl walked into the light and sat at the table, facing Salina. Salina was stunned by the girl's green eyes and red hair. Salina's people all had brown eyes and black hair. She had never seen anyone with eyes like that, the color of a pine tree glistening with dew in the morning sun. They were mesmerizing.

The woman broke the silence. "Are you joining our coven?"

"Coven? What's a coven?"

"It's a group."

"A group? Like a tribe?"

The woman shrugged. "I guess it could be a sort of tribe."

"I don't really have any place to go, so…"

"Then I guess you're staying here for now." The woman rose, filled a bowl with something cooking on the fire, and sat back down. "There used to be four of us but Oma banished one before the last full moon. Right after that, she said she was going to get a new coven member, and here you are."

Salina tried to remember the details of the night she'd met Oma. She could barely remember talking to her, and certainly couldn't remember anything about joining a…coven? "No, you must be mistaken. I left my tribe and have not found a new one yet."

"Oh, you've found a new one, all right. You were handpicked by Oma herself. What did she ask you for?" The woman shoveled a spoonful of whatever was in the bowl into her mouth.

"Ask me for? She didn't ask me for anything."

"She must have asked you for something before you came here."

Salina nodded. "Yes, she asked me for payment

in exchange for a potion I needed."

"That's what she told you? A potion in exchange for a price?" The woman wiped food from the corner of her mouth with the back of her hand, then threw her head back and laughed. "You just don't understand yet. She doesn't need anything from you. She could give you a potion out of the kindness of her heart, except for the fact she has no heart and wouldn't know kindness. The price she asked you for was to get you here. You were chosen to replace the banished one."

"What does banish mean?"

"When it comes to Oma, one is never quite sure. She simply gets rid of you. You could be burned, killed, drowned, or maybe just sent away. We never find out those kinds of things, but when Oma makes up her mind, you're just gone. So, my advice to you is, you need to do as Oma wishes or you will find yourself in the same predicament."

"What would Oma ask of me? And what if I don't want to stay here?"

The woman smiled a mischievous smile, then flipped her long red hair over her shoulder. "You'll stay. You already said you have no choice. As far as what she will ask of you, well, you never know. It could be anything." The woman pushed away her bowl. She stood up and wrapped herself in a black cloak like the one Oma wore, pulling the hood over her red hair. She walked toward the stone wall and waved her hand through the air. An opening appeared, and on the other side was the forest. She turned back to Salina. "Whatever it is, don't say no." She walked through the opening as if it were a door that had always been there. The opening then vanished, reverting to stone.

Salina ran to the wall. She felt around but did not feel an opening, not even a breeze.

"Oh, don't worry about her," Oma said from behind her.

Salina spun around, startled.

"She's just upset that I banished her sister. And she's probably a little jealous of you since you gave me what she couldn't. She's not very powerful and she knows it."

"But she just opened a rock and walked through it!"

She blew a hiss of air between her teeth. "Means nothing." Oma reached into her cloak and produced an apple. "Here, I brought you this."

Salina cautiously took it from her.

"Eat something and then I'll introduce you to the other women."

Chapter 19

Karma

Margaret remained still, barely breathing, standing in the hallway outside the kitchen door. The old women continued their hushed conversation.

"She has to know the whole truth if we stand any chance of getting her daughter back," Myrtle whispered.

"I agree she needs to know what's going on, but she doesn't need to know everything," Ivy countered.

"Ivy, we need her. You know we do. We're out of practice. After all these years and everything we've tried, we've never been able to get them out. We've only been able to save one."

There was silence, and Margaret hoped they hadn't stopped talking because they realized she was there.

Finally, Grandma Ivy said, "And I don't want to lose that one. He's too important to me."

The screen door slammed as Rich entered the house.

"Hey," he said when he saw Margaret, "are you feeling better?"

Margaret took a step forward and then spun around to face him, as if she had just been walking toward the kitchen and was not eavesdropping on the old women. "Yes, I'm sorry I overreacted."

"Oh, don't be sorry. I probably would have

acted the same way." Rich smiled as they entered the kitchen together.

After a short and awkwardly quiet supper of corn bread and lima beans, Myrtle rose from her chair. "Well, I should be going back to my hotel now. It's been a very long day."

"Why don't you stay here with us?" Rich asked.

"I've lived alone for a very long time. I like my privacy. I'll see you tomorrow." She turned to Margaret. "Get Ivy to tell you all about the mounds. You must learn about the history if you are to believe anything I tell you."

Margaret nodded.

Myrtle turned to Grandma Ivy. "Don't dillydally."

Myrtle was already out the door before anyone thought to offer to walk her out. Rich and Margaret stared at Grandma Ivy, who rose to begin clearing the dishes from the table.

"Don't dillydally? What does that mean?" Rich asked.

Grandma Ivy placed a stack of plates in the sink. "It means we should get to bed early. We have a very busy day tomorrow. Will you both finish clearing the supper dishes?"

"Of course, we will," Margaret said.

"Thank you," Grandma Ivy said as she walked toward the kitchen door. "Good night, children."

"Goodnight, Grandma," Rich said.

Margaret sat back down as soon as Grandma Ivy had left the room. "Rich, we need to talk," she whispered.

"Sure." He placed the glasses in the sink and returned to the table. "What's on your mind?"

"You need to sit down for a minute and listen. There's something strange going on here. Something we don't know about. I think these women actually know where Sarah is."

Rich shook his head. "How could they possibly know that? I know they've been filling your head with crazy stuff about witches, but their stories are simply too farfetched. I'm beginning to think they might just be crazy old women."

She paused, weighing her options, but knew she had to tell him. "I heard them talking about getting others back, and they said they've only been able to get one."

"Back from where? I'm not following."

"Back from the kidnappers or whatever they are."

Rich thumbed over his shoulder. "Them? Getting children back? When? In 1861?" He chuckled. "Maggie, I think they're getting to you."

The look on her face told him she was serious. "Rich, what year were you born?"

"Same as you. Seventy-eight."

"What happened to your parents?"

"I don't know. I've always lived with my grandma."

She looked at him.

"I'm still not following. What does this have to do with your daughter?"

"I think Grandma Ivy was right. I'm beginning to think Sarah is just another in a long line of missing children. The last missing since 1978."

Rich's face turned pale.

Lori Crane

Chapter 20

Coven

Salina sank into a deep depression and didn't speak much during the first few weeks with Oma, but there were two other women besides the redhead who kept coaxing Salina to cheer up.

"Why are you so sad?" the skinny brunette asked repeatedly.

After much persuading, Salina finally told them her story. "I lost my child and I almost died. Oma gave me a potion to recover, but the price I had to pay her was too high. In exchange for the potion, I lost my family and my husband. I would rather be dead."

"Oh, nonsense," quipped the black-haired girl. "You can have any family, any husband, any baby you want. You are immortal. You can have many families."

Salina gawked at her in disbelief. "As if families and children were a commodity to collect."

The black-haired girl stirred the food cooking in the black pot. "Well, not collect, but you can certainly have those things if you desire. Look at Oma; she desires a child, and she gets a child. She asked for a baby for a very long time, but we didn't know how to get her one. It's a good thing you came along and got a baby for her. She's much happier now. You probably wouldn't like Oma when she's not happy. She can be a very dark witch."

"She may be happy, but my sister Mia is not."

The brunette spoke. "You'll find most mortals are not happy, even when they have everything their heart desires. We've been around for generations and have witnessed sadness in mortals forever."

Salina's interest was piqued. "How long have you been here with Oma?"

"I've been here since before your people came to this area," the black-haired woman said.

"And I've been with Oma for longer than that," the brunette said. "We used to live north of here, where the ground is often covered in ice and snow. We came here about five hundred years ago. There was a couple more with us at the time: the girl you met when you first got here, her sister, and another who, at the time, was the leader of the coven."

"A different leader than Oma? What happened to her?" Salina asked.

The two women glanced at each other. The brunette spoke in a hushed tone. "Oma didn't like her much. She arranged to have a landslide bury her."

"But aren't you immortal?"

"Yes, we are, but we can still be murdered if it's done the right way. It has to be instantaneous. You need to prove yourself of some use so Oma doesn't do the same thing to you."

"What kind of use can I be?"

"You never know. Oma will let you know when it's time," the brunette said.

The black-haired girl added, "And it's best to do as Oma wishes. You don't want to rebel against her or stand up to her."

"You can't stand up to her. It's impossible," the brunette added as she ladled some food into a bowl and handed it to Salina.

Salina took the bowl. "What do you do for her?"

"Anything she wishes," they said in unison.

Salina took a bite of the hot food. It was very good. "I'm sorry, I don't even know your names."

The girls looked at each other and didn't answer.

"Do you have names?" Salina asked.

"You couldn't even pronounce them if we told them to you," said the brunette.

"Yes, and it doesn't really matter what our names are. You can call us whatever you'd like. Oma does," said the black-haired girl.

Lori Crane

Chapter 21

Hints

After Margaret went to bed, Rich sat in the kitchen with his laptop. The light of the screen surrounded him as he tried to wrap his head around what Margaret had told him. It was impossible, wasn't it? Of course, it was. Ivy was his grandmother. His parents had died when he was an infant. There was no more to his history than that. These missing children had nothing to do with him. A boy had disappeared in 1978. So, what? It was a coincidence. Still, he emailed the sheriff, asking for information on the child from 1978. He received an almost immediate response.

"Hi Rich,

The only information I have on that missing child are the names of the family members and the locations of the initial searches. The child was never found. I've scanned these old documents and have attached what I have for you. I'm thinking this case needs to be closed, as it was over thirty-nine years ago, there isn't any family to speak of anymore, and I see no reason to continue the investigation. I'm going to wait and see what happens in the case of Sarah Speedwell before I decide.

According to the file I've attached, it seems the father was the first on the list of suspects, but it turned out he was with his family when the event occurred and had no history whatsoever of violence or run-ins with the law. He was eliminated as a suspect early on.

About a month after the disappearance, the mother committed suicide, and the father subsequently disappeared. Apparently, he took to the bottle. The remaining twin went into the foster-care system and was bounced around from family to family until he was sixteen, when he ran away from his foster home. He was never adopted. The other day, after you brought this case to my attention, I looked into the father's whereabouts and found he lived on the streets for a while before drinking himself to death. He died in 1980.

Let me know if you need anything else. I guess you're writing a piece on the disappearances. Good luck with it. Please tell Mrs. Speedwell I'm sorry she was so distressed tonight. I never meant to upset her. I'll give her a call in the next day or so and give her an update on the search. I spoke with Mr. Speedwell after I got home. He said their other daughter still isn't speaking. I don't know if we'll ever find out what happened out there. I'm not feeling very encouraged at this point. It's been almost three weeks, and we have no leads. If it was an abduction, we'd have something, anything to go on at this point. If the child wandered away, this would certainly be a recovery mission by now. It's definitely keeping me up at night deciding how long to continue the search.

Well, good night. Let me know if you need anything else.
Andy Miller

Rich opened the attached file.

The family's name was Flint—Joseph and Betty Flint. Their boys were Joseph Jr. and Raymond, apparently named after Betty's father. The handwritten police report of the disappearance stated the family had been enjoying a picnic at the Bynum Mounds with the six-month-old twins resting together in a playpen. The father wandered into the woods to relieve himself and the mother took one of the boys to the car to change his diaper. The remaining twin was asleep in the playpen, alone in the field. When both parents returned, the infant was gone. The parents' statements were identical. No one else was at the mounds that day. Neither of them heard or saw anything or anyone. Joe Jr. never cried.

Rich looked through the dark kitchen window. In the distance, a pale light shone on the peak of the barn. "No trace," he mumbled to himself, "just like Sarah." He'd love to know about the case in 1943. "I'd bet money on it," he said to himself, thinking there would be no trace of that child, either. Maybe Grandma Ivy was on to something. Children didn't just disappear without a trace, yet these children seemed to follow the same pattern. And though he told Margaret he thought the old women were crazy, his gut told him there was definitely something going on between his grandmother and that Myrtle woman. He couldn't quite put his finger on it, but knew they had secrets between them. Maybe Grandma Ivy would explain it all in the morning.

He looked at the clock on his computer. It was late. He should get to bed. Morning would arrive soon enough.

Before he called it a day, there was one more thing he wanted to check. He closed the files from the sheriff and googled the name Raymond Flint. The top of the search results read RAYMOND FLINT, ATTORNEY AT LAW. He clicked on it.

The website was for a lawyer in Memphis who specialized in drunk driving, medical malpractice, hit-and-run. "An ambulance chaser."

He clicked the ABOUT THE FIRM tab, which opened a drop-down menu. The top choice read MEET RAYMOND.

Amid some grandiose claims about getting every dollar possible for the firm's clients, there was a picture of a man that could have been a mirror image of Rich.

He didn't move for the next hour.

Chapter 22

Kidnapping

Oma looked up when the women stomped into the cave, their footfall echoing off the damp walls.

They stopped in front of Oma and glared at her.

Oma wasn't surprised. These two had been trouble since the day they came to live with her.

"What is it?" she snapped.

"We want you to stop," one said.

"Stop what?"

"You know very well what," the second woman said.

Oma sighed and rose from her chair. What had happened to the day when her subordinates were respectful? She was tired of disposing of them. First the red-haired girl, now these two, who were numbers sixteen and seventeen. The only one left who had any manners was Salina.

Oma walked toward the back of the cave to gather her cloak. "I really don't have time for your riddles. I have things to do." She breezed past them, wrapping her cloak around her shoulders.

As she neared the opening of the cave, the first one yelled, "Stop right there!"

Oma froze. The only sound was a small, gray mouse in the corner, crunching on a crumb. The air felt as if it had turned to ice. Then, like an approaching storm, complete with black clouds and rumbling thunder, Oma turned to face the women. "Did you just raise your voice to me?"

The women remained motionless and didn't respond.

Oma walked toward them and stopped an inch from the brunette's face. She spoke in a measured tone. "What makes you think you can speak to me in such a manner?"

"I...I'm sorry, Oma, but we need to discuss something with you," the brunette said in a near whisper.

Oma cocked her head toward the black-haired girl. "You both need to discuss something with me? What could you possibly need to discuss with me?"

The women simultaneously stuttered something unintelligible.

"One at a time, please. You'd better say what you have to say and quickly. I don't have all day."

The brunette cleared her throat. "Oma." She paused. "Oma, we want you to stop taking babies."

Oma huffed. "You what?"

The brunette swallowed hard. "Yes, Oma, we want to ask you to not take any more children. We've seen the children's families destroyed. They're just brokenhearted even after much time passes. They're so sad. It's not fair."

"Fair to whom? And since when are you allowed to ask me to do or not do anything? I am the leader of this coven, the ruler of everything around you, the master of all you see. You have no say in anything that happens here. Whatever you want is irrelevant."

The brunette looked at the floor for a moment then back at Oma. "But don't you see how sad their mothers are? You send Salina out to…to do your dirty work. It makes her sad, too."

"Dirty work?" Oma bellowed. "What sort of statement is that?"

"You do see the sadness. I know you do. That's why you don't have the guts to steal a child yourself. That's why you send Salina to do it. You know she's afraid of you, so she does anything you tell her to. And every couple of decades you send her for another one. Once the child is grown, you dump them somewhere, sometimes alive, sometimes dead. It doesn't matter to you. You're just playing with them. But you must also know that you're playing with real people. Real people with real feelings. You're destroying lives and families and children. We want you to stop!"

Oma didn't move.

The women didn't either. They barely breathed.

It felt like the entire cave shook when Oma thundered, "SALINA!"

A moment later, Salina took a step forward from the back of the cave. The tension in the room was as thick as soup. "Yes, Oma?" she asked nervously.

"Come here."

"Yes, Oma." Salina approached Oma and stood by her side, not looking at the other two women.

"Salina, tell these traitors you are not afraid of me."

Salina softly said, "I am not afraid of Oma."

"Tell them you don't mind taking children for me."

"I don't mind t…t…taking ch…childre…"

"Tell them!"

"I don't mind t…t…" She turned to Oma. "I can't."

"You can't what?"

"I can't say that. I am many things, but I am not a liar. I cannot say it."

"Are you saying you'd rather be out in the woods where I found you two hundred years ago? I've given you warmth and comfort, and I gave you this family"—she snarled at the pair— "such that it is."

Salina bowed her head. "Thank you for everything you do for me, Oma. I'm not worthy of your generosity."

A wicked grin came across Oma's face. "This conversation has me suddenly longing for another child. Salina, you can repay my kindness by bringing me one." She turned to the others, her nose rising into the air. "And you two can repay me by keeping your mouths shut." Her grin faded. "I'm not interested in what you think or what you want. If you don't like it, you're more than welcome to leave." She turned back to Salina. "I'll expect to see a new babe here within the next few days. It's been a long time since we've had a baby in the coven." She left the cave.

The brunette asked, "Salina, where's Myrtle?"

"She's gathering blackberries down at the creek."

"Do you think she could talk some sense into Oma?"

"No, she won't stand up to Oma. Why would you want her to do that?"

"It just seems with her firsthand experience of being taken from her mother, she might be able to help Oma understand."

Salina lowered her head and mumbled, "No, she won't help you. I won't allow it. I protect Myrtle like she's my own child. I will not allow her to stand up to Oma."

Salina walked to the back of the cave and disappeared into a dark hallway.

Chapter 23

Confessions

Margaret sat alone with Grandma Ivy at the kitchen table, the late morning sun hidden by gray, low-hanging clouds. The humidity was on the rise, and when the afternoon heat increased, the day would become unbearably damp and sticky. Grandma Ivy patted the back of her neck with a white, lace-edged handkerchief. Margaret stared out the window at the willow tree hanging limply near the pond. Not even the birds were moving today. The air was too heavy for them to exert the energy.

The women were waiting for Rich to get up. So far, they hadn't heard any sounds from him. Uncharacteristically, he seemed to be sleeping in this morning. Perhaps the lack of sunshine was allowing him to get the rest he needed. Margaret wished she could do the same. She was tired. But as the clocked ticked the minutes away, she grew more and more anxious to start the day.

"Grandma Ivy, I can't wait any longer. I'm ready to learn and understand what Myrtle is talking about. She said I need to know the history of the Bynum Mounds, so let's start there. What do you know about it?"

Grandma Ivy sighed. "Okay, but it's a very long story. It's going to take us a while to get through it in a manner that you will understand." She looked out the window. "It all began about two thousand years ago."

She told Margaret about the ancient Natives who'd lived in the area, about the wife of the chief who'd lost her child, about the wife of the chief's brother who had given birth to twins. "The chief's wife was named Salina."

There was something wistful in her eyes when she said the name, but Margaret didn't interrupt to ask why that was.

"The brother's wife was named Mia," Grandma Ivy continued.

"Wait! Mia? Myrtle said I look like someone named Mia. That can't be the same Mia, can it? How would she possibly know what that Mia looked like?"

Ivy breathed in and said, "They've met."

"That's not possible."

"I assure you it is."

Margaret shook her head.

"Let me explain further," the old woman said.

She continued the story, telling of how Oma tricked Salina into stealing one of Mia's infants, and how Salina was forced to leave the tribe in order to save her husband's dignity. "So, Salina joined the coven."

"A coven? Like a witches' coven? Are those the witches you and Myrtle have been talking about?"

Ivy nodded.

"Wait. How could you possibly know all this?"

"Dear, I know this is going to be nearly impossible for you to believe, but what do you remember about me and this house from your childhood?"

"I remember almost everything. Nothing here has changed since I was a child. Not even you."

"It hasn't changed because I make sure it

doesn't change. Every detail of my life here is perfectly orchestrated to remain exactly the same, as to avoid questions, to stay discreet, to be an inconspicuous grandmother in an unremarkable house, living an ordinary life."

"What are you talking about?"

Ivy looked into Margaret's eyes. "I'm an immortal, Margaret. In your world, I guess I would be called a witch."

Now it was Margaret's turn to pause.

Ivy gave her a moment to accept the revelation. "It's true. Myrtle and I have been friends for many, many years. Much the way everyone else joined the coven, I have my story, too. That day I was at the mounds with my mother and my sister, and she and my grandmother were arguing?"

"Yes?"

"I ran behind the trees to keep from hearing them yell at each other. I was really frightened, as I had never, ever heard my grandmother raise her voice before. I was taken that day by Salina. Not my sister, just me. Salina didn't really kidnap me; I went willingly. She transformed herself to looked like a little girl, and she coaxed me to run and play with her. By the time I realized I was lost in the woods and very far from my mother, it was too late. I didn't know my way back. Salina told me to come home with her, and I did.

"After many years, Oma allowed me to see my family. She took me to a hospital where my mother lived. It was a psychiatric hospital. I don't know for certain, but I think she was admitted after I ran off, or was taken, depending on how you look at it. I was shocked when I saw her. When I left my mother, she had been a young, beautiful woman, but this woman before me was a senile, old lady. She had aged, but I hadn't aged at the same pace. I was afraid to speak with her, so I watched her from a distance, so saddened that she was not the mother I remembered. A middle-aged woman came to see her, and I recognized the woman instantly as my twin sister. But I didn't understand how she was so much older than me. I was still young. I finally worked up the courage to approach my sister and say hello. She didn't recognize me. Our mother didn't know me, either. I didn't tell them, as I knew they'd never believe me, and I couldn't possibly explain it. I couldn't comprehend it myself. All I knew was these people were not my family anymore. These people were complete strangers. I had no family.

"Myrtle held me that night as I cried, releasing my fantasies of someday going home to my real family. Myrtle was good to me. She had pretty much been the one who raised me, and she was the only person who understood my sadness, for she had been taken from her mother also.

"She said she had seen her mother, too. She had run across her mother in the woods many years after she was taken, but by then her mother had given birth to many more children who were, at the time, all nearly grown. Her mother seemed to have a full and rich life. Myrtle changed her appearance and approached her mother and made small talk. She said her mother's expression was one of hopelessness, her eyes full of pain and heartache. She was surrounded by a large and loving family, but her spirit was sad. She never got over losing her infant."

Ivy stopped, took a deep breath, and exhaled, the corners of her mouth turned down. "From what I understand, Salina protected Mia's baby as she grew.

Oma tended to dispose of children once they grew up, but Salina would have given her life to keep that child safe. She stole some of Oma's potion and gave it to the child. Oma never found out. When I was brought into the coven, Myrtle protected me in the same way. That is why she is my oldest and dearest friend."

Margaret didn't know what to say. Either this was an insane fabrication or the saddest story she had ever heard in her life. Considering how she was feeling about Sarah, she understood how a mother could completely fall apart after losing a child, even end up in an asylum. Margaret was barely hanging on herself. "Your mother must have been devastated. It's no wonder she never recovered. She never found out what happened to her baby."

Ivy nodded. "After the hospital visit to see my mother, Myrtle and I tried to convince Oma to stop taking children, but she wouldn't listen to us. She told us we reminded her of some other girls who used to be in the coven, girls who voiced opinions that weren't welcome. She threatened us, telling us she killed those girls and she would kill us too if we ever brought it up again. We decided to go to Salina, since she was the one who took the first child and was Oma's puppet who continued taking children each time Oma requested one. We asked her to stop, but she wouldn't stand up to Oma. Still won't."

"Wait. This is too much. So, you're telling me you're a witch, like with a pointy hat and a broom and a coven?" Margaret's tone dripped with sarcasm.

"No hats, no brooms, and Myrtle and I left the coven thirty-nine years ago."

Margaret buried her face in her hands and mumbled through her fingers. "I'm so confused. I think

I'm losing my mind." She looked back up. "This story is completely impossible. You both led me to believe you knew where my daughter was. I'm wasting my time here." She rose from the chair.

"You're not wasting your time, Margaret. Please sit back down and listen." Her tone was stern.

Margaret remained standing. "You can tell me one thing. What does any of this have to do with my daughter?"

"I'm getting to that. I'm afraid there are details in this story that will probably ruin my family, so you'll need to excuse me for being hesitant." She cleared her throat. "I realize you need to learn the truth to save your daughter, but this is very difficult."

"Missing my daughter is very difficult, too. Can you please get to the point?"

Ivy gestured to the chair.

"I'll give you five more minutes." Margaret sat down, her back rigid.

Ivy continued. "Oma was the head of our coven, and from all the stories I ever heard about her, she always had a desire to have a child by her side. I guess it made her feel loved or something. Of course, being witches, we can't have our own children, so we need to get them from elsewhere. So, the very first child she took was Mia's daughter."

"Yeah, I already know that part."

"But there's something you don't know. You know Mia's daughter."

Margaret shook her head.

"Her name is Myrtle."

It was as if all the air had been sucked out of the room. Margaret closed her eyes and willed the room to stop spinning.

"I know this is hard to comprehend, Margaret."

Margaret opened her eyes. "This is impossible to comprehend! First you tell me you're a witch, not even bothering to question whether I actually believe in witches, which I don't. Now you're telling me the woman I spoke with yesterday is two thousand years old."

Ivy remained silent, allowing Margaret to process the information. Margaret stared at the tabletop.

"Wait." Margaret looked at Ivy. "How old are you? You look exactly the same as you did when I was a child."

Ivy smiled faintly. "I am whatever age I choose to be." She gestured to her face. "This is the age I chose to become a grandmother to Rich. I don't get any questions from the community. I don't have men calling on me. I'm just an old woman in an old farmhouse in the country, not bothering anyone."

Margaret placed her hand over her mouth, not taking her eyes off Ivy.

Ivy stared back at Margaret. "I guess I need to prove it to you."

"I don't want to see you change into a different age. I'm barely hanging on to sanity right now."

"How about something less scary, then?" Ivy waved her hand over the wilted daisies in the middle of the table, and their drooping white petals instantly plumped up. The green leaves lifted and spread wide.

Margaret's jaw fell open. "How did you do that?"

"That's nothing. Just a parlor trick."

"So, you can do other things?"

"I can do just about anything I want. So, can

Myrtle. Do you need more proof?"

Margaret shook her head, her jaw still slack.

"Back to the story, then. Okay?"

Margaret nodded.

"Myrtle remained Oma's child until the age of thirteen, and then, thanks to Salina stealing Oma's potion, she joined the coven and became immortal. Oma never said a word about it. Over the decades, Oma took more children, but she never kept another one like she kept Myrtle. Sometimes they died in her care. Sometimes she dumped them near a distant village to never be seen again. Of all the children over all those years, there was never another who grew up to become a member of the coven, until I came along.

"Myrtle used to disappear for long periods of time, and Salina found out she was following her mother in the woods. She'd sit at a distance and watch Mia gathering berries or working in the village garden. She watched her twin with her mother, and she longed to be with them. She had missed growing up with her family. But she couldn't return to them, not without an explanation of where she had been for years, and without aging as a normal person would.

"One time, she threatened to go back to her family, and Oma told her she'd kill them all and destroy their entire village if she did. She threatened to kill Myrtle's mother if Myrtle ever even mentioned it again. Myrtle never said anything else about her family to anyone. When Mia died of old age, Myrtle snuck out to see her one last time. She creeped into the hut where Mia had been entombed in a cypress box. She opened the box and placed copper bracelets on her mother's wrists. One for her and one for her twin. As far as I know, the box was never opened after that, and Mia was cremated on the mounds with those bracelets on her wrists.

"That day, while Myrtle stood at the back of the crowd, watching them light the box on fire, Oma sent Salina out to take another child. Myrtle was furious when she returned and found the child, but she couldn't do anything about it. Over the decades, each time Salina stole another child, Myrtle's anger grew. She grew to hate Oma and vowed someday to exact her revenge. Myrtle attempted to get various children away from Oma, but she never succeeded. Oma stopped her every time, but unlike the others Oma killed, she never punished Myrtle.

"Eventually I came along and Myrtle took care of me. It was almost as if we were a happy family. Then the day came when Salina stole another child. Myrtle confided in me that she would never let Oma destroy another family. She asked me to help her get the child away from Oma. I knew she was right. We needed to do something to stop this cycle. We didn't really have a plan. Oma was deadly strong, but we had to try.

"We grabbed the baby in the middle of the night and ran as fast as we could. We were afraid Oma would kill us when she caught us, but when she finally tracked us down, the only thing she did was kick us out of the coven. She said she would someday get even with us, and it would be enjoyable observing us awaiting reckoning, as we would live in the fear of never knowing when the retribution was to occur. She was set on toying with us as long as her patience would allow.

"After we saved the child, Myrtle and I split up. I took the child here to Tupelo. Myrtle went to Meridian. We haven't talked or seen each other for years, thirty-nine years. You know, over the years, I began to think Oma might have been lying to us the entire time. She had always told us she was the one who gave us immortality and she was the one who could turn us into dust. But if that were true, then why hasn't she done so? Maybe she can't. I do feel bad for Salina, though. She's still with her."

"Wait. Oma and Salina are still alive?"

"Why, of course they are. They are just as alive today as Myrtle and I."

"So, what happened to the baby you saved from Oma?"

The front screen door slammed, making Margaret jump. Rich stormed into the kitchen, looking like a wild man. He was unshaven, his hair tousled, his eyes red.

Margaret opened her mouth to say, "I thought you were still sleeping," but she was cut off.

"I've just spent hours at the county building where I've failed to convince them there should be some kind of records for a person named Rich Martin. There are no records! Not even a birth certificate. No record of a Mr. and Mrs. Martin dying in 1978. No adoption records. No family. Nothing! You," he pointed at Ivy, "have some explaining to do."

Ivy's face turned ghostly white.

"Well?" Rich yelled.

Ivy looked at Margaret and softly said, "I'm not sure you want to be here for this conversation, dear."

"I'm staying right here." She turned to Rich. "How is that possible?"

"How much has she told you?"

"She's told me more than I can even comprehend. Do you know the story?"

"The only thing I know is this woman is not my grandmother."

Ivy groaned.

"Why did you keep me? Why didn't you return me to my family?"

Margaret had a sudden realization. "Ivy, is Rich the child you saved from Oma?"

Ivy didn't respond.

Rich glared at her.

Ivy nodded.

Margaret gasped.

"Who's Oma?" Rich asked.

"That's a long story," Margaret said.

"Sit down, boy, and I'll tell you what happened," Ivy said.

"I don't think there can possibly be an excuse for what you've done to my life and my family," Rich said as he reluctantly sat in the nearest chair.

"I don't expect you to ever understand, but the truth is, by the time we rescued you, your mother had already died and your father went off the deep end and drank himself to death. We tried to return you to your family, but by the time we got you away from Oma, there was no family left."

"Who's we?"

"Myrtle and I."

"Myrtle? What does she have to do with this? You said I'd know her, but I've never seen her before in my life."

"I'll start again from the beginning."

Lori Crane

Chapter 24

Banished

A monstrous storm was brewing.

The tall skinny pine trees bent in the strong winds. The sky was pitch-black. The storm clouds hung over the land like a wet blanket. It was nearly impossible for Myrtle and Ivy to see where they were going, but they knew the way through the forest by heart. They kept running, stumbling over roots, branches scratching their arms. The trees groaned in protest as the howling winds surrounded Myrtle and Ivy like ferocious animals.

"Hurry," Myrtle urged.

"I'm going as fast as I can." Ivy was puffing with each step.

The baby boy in her arms, jostled and tossed, didn't make a sound, as if he knew his very life depended upon his silence.

"I think she's behind us," Myrtle said.

"Don't look back," Ivy warned.

Thunder sounded, shaking the land. Lightning lit the path before them, striking a tree just ahead. The bark exploded and disintegrated, leaving only a cloud of dust that instantly blew away.

"Stop!" Myrtle screamed.

Ivy did. "Why? What is it?"

"Did you see something ahead?"

"No, what did you see?"

175

"I think it's her."

"It can't be. She doesn't even know we're gone."

Myrtle was trembling and staring straight ahead. "She knows everything."

"Not this, she doesn't. We have to get away from here now. Let's go." Ivy moved forward again.

Lightning crackled, spreading its electric fingers in all directions. That's when they saw her. Oma stood motionless on the path, blocking the entrance to the field.

"What do we do?" Myrtle asked.

A clap of thunder resounded, making both women jump.

"It's no use. We're going to have to face her," Ivy said in a more confident tone than she felt.

"She'll kill us."

Ivy took a step forward. "Then so be it."

The light of a torch appeared in the opening of the field. Oma was holding it. She turned and carried it to the center of the field.

Ivy marched forward, refusing to cower to this woman any longer.

"Where do you think you're going?" Oma bellowed as Myrtle and Ivy emerged from the forest. Oma stopped in the middle of the field, slammed the torch into the ground, and turned to face them.

"We've had enough of this, Oma. We're not going to let you take any more children!" Ivy didn't slow as she approached Oma. She would either collide with Oma or walk right through her, but she was determined to keep moving forward with this child.

"Stop!" roared Oma when Ivy was about one hundred yards in front of her.

Ivy did not stop. Myrtle slowed, staying behind Ivy.

"Stop, I said!"

When Oma took a step back, Ivy's courage grew. "We will not stop! We will not listen to you any longer," she yelled over the roaring winds.

They were only a few yards apart now. The fire in the torch danced wildly. Oma grabbed the fire with her bare hands and held it threateningly over her head. "Stop!"

"If you're going to throw that fire at us, you'd better do so quickly. Then move out of our way," Ivy commanded.

Oma's face glowed blood red in the light. Her cloak billowed around her. "I told you if you ever crossed me, I would kill you. Did you not hear me?"

"If you're going to kill us, do so!"

"You're not taking that child."

"Oh, yes, we are." Ivy passed Oma without incident and kept walking. It couldn't be this easy. Oma must be up to something, but Ivy didn't have time to imagine what that might be. She kept moving. She had to get this boy to safety.

"And what will you do now that I have your friend?"

Ivy turned and saw Oma holding Myrtle around her neck with one arm, the other still holding the fireball in the air.

"Let her go!" Ivy screamed.

"Give me the child back."

No one moved.

Oma changed her voice to a syrupy tone. "Give me the child and I'll let your friend go. A life for a life."

Ivy weighed her options. As if rushing her to

decide, thunder shook the ground.

Myrtle had turned pale. "Go, Ivy, go! She can do whatever she wants to…" Her words were cut off by a clawed hand around her throat.

Ivy remained still.

"Let her go!" an additional voice demanded from behind Oma.

Salina emerged from the forest.

Oma threw Myrtle to the ground as she turned toward Salina. "Are you going to join them? After all I've done for you, are you really going to turn against me now?"

Salina walked toward Oma as if taking a leisurely stroll on a beach. No hesitation. No hurry.

Myrtle crawled toward Ivy. Ivy helped her to her feet.

"Are you okay?" she whispered to Myrtle.

Myrtle nodded, rubbing her neck, which was red with welts and watery blisters that were growing by the second.

Salina stopped a few inches in front of Oma. "Oma, I'm not going to join them, but they've been trying to run away for long enough. Let them go. We will start a new coven with women who don't cause so much trouble."

Oma turned to Myrtle and Ivy. "They're not taking my child!"

The hair on the back of Ivy's neck stood up. "He's not your child! I was not your child. Myrtle was not your child. All those children you so conveniently disposed of when they grew old enough to question you—those were not your children. You don't have any children of your own. You're a dried up, shriveled, old hag who is not capable of having children or loving children or raising children!"

"I raised you." She pointed toward Myrtle. "I raised her."

"We were not yours to raise, Oma! We were taken from our real mothers, from our real families, from our real lives. We were taken for some sick and twisted reason that only you can explain. We are taking this child, we're returning him to his family, and we're leaving you for good. You've ruined our lives. You've ruined our families' lives. We're not going to stand by and watch you ruin any more lives, ever! This is finished right here, right now."

Oma was quaking in anger. She slowly placed the fire back onto the top of the torch.

As if on cue, the storm stopped abruptly. The wind quieted. The thunder and lightning and gray clouds vanished. Time stood still as the women faced each other across the field.

Oma pointed at Myrtle. "I told you the last time you tried to take my child I would kill you if you ever rose against me again."

No tree frogs sang. No coyotes howled. The land was silent.

Oma continued, "I told you I would rip your heart out and feed it to the coyotes."

She raised her hand toward the woods and a coyote howled. Within seconds, a few others joined in the chorus.

"I told you the next time you did something against me, you would regret it."

Ivy was sure Oma was about to kill them. Salina stood behind Oma, nervously biting her fingernails.

Suddenly Oma's black cloak lifted as if a wind had grabbed it, but there was no wind. Her black hair flew around her. She spun, as though caught in a tornado. As she rose into the air, she became a ball of fire, growing taller and wider with each spin. A demonic voice roared from the center of the fireball, which had reached fifteen feet tall. "I told you next time I would kill you!"

"RUN!" Myrtle yelled as she turned and fled across the field.

"NO! Stop!" Ivy yelled. "I'm through running. We will finish this here and now. Oma, your show of power has always been terrifying to us, but I'm not afraid of you anymore. I'm done with living in fear of you. If you want to kill me, then go ahead and do so!" Ivy handed the child to Myrtle, who backed away, shielding the baby. She spread her arms wide as she took a step toward the ball of flames. "Come on, Oma." She took another step. "Go ahead." One more step.

The fiery ball inched toward Ivy.

"Come on, Oma. What are you waiting for? Let's do this!" Ivy said. Another step.

"You will die!" the flame growled.

"Maybe. But you'll never know until you try." Another step.

"You...will...die!" The massive flames roared as a fireball flew toward Ivy's head.

Ivy deflected it with her right wrist.

Oma threw another, fast as lightning.

Ivy ducked. "Is that all you have? Fireballs?" Ivy waved her arm and created a waterfall out of thin air. Blue water poured from an invisible source, splashing everything around it.

That startled Oma for a moment. Then it angered her. Her fiery tornado grew louder and larger.

Twenty feet into the air now. "You...will...die!" Oma shook the field, just as the thunder had done only a moment ago.

"No, not today!" Ivy grabbed a ball of water from the waterfall and threw it at Oma.

It sizzled and evaporated when it hit the fire, causing a small cloud of steam to rise.

Oma's laugh was deep. "Is that all you've got?"

"No, it's not."

Oma paused.

Shafts of blue light, like fingers of lightning bolts, emerged from the center of the giant fireball that was Oma, spreading snakes of electricity in every direction. Oma trembled and looked down at her stomach. She had been impaled from behind by the torch that had been staked in the ground. Her torch. She spun around, breaking the torch in half, and glared at Salina, who stood with the bottom half of the torch in her hands. "Why? Why do you fight me?"

Salina spoke like a mother trying to calm a toddler having a tantrum. "You need to let them go. They are no good to us."

Oma's expression turned from rage to curiosity. "Us? You've never said the word *us* before."

"Yes, us. You are my family, Oma. You are my mother, my friend. If you let them go, we can be happy together, just the two of us."

The fiery whirlwind slowed and dimmed, becoming simply Oma once again.

Salina remained in her spot, still holding the end of the torch.

Oma took a step toward her. "Happy?"

"Yes, we could be." Salina smiled.

Behind Oma, Ivy waved her hand and the

waterfall vanished. Oma didn't notice.

"Oma, please, just let them go."

The fire surrounding Oma changed from red to blue and finally disappeared. "Are you sure?"

"Yes." Salina dropped the end of the torch.

"Really?"

"Really."

Oma turned to Myrtle and Ivy. "Go!"

Myrtle and Ivy didn't move.

"Did you hear me?" Her voice grew louder. "Go before I change my mind."

Myrtle and Ivy backed up slowly.

"GO!" Oma yelled.

They both turned and ran.

Oma's voice followed them. "Wherever your feet touch the ground, no grass will ever grow. If I ever change my mind, I will find you."

Chapter 25

Truth

"So, what's the plan?" Margaret blurted out, without so much as a good morning to the ladies drinking coffee at the table. "And where's Rich?" She noticed the sun sneaking in through the edge of the west window and glanced at the clock above the sink. It was already half past noon. How did she sleep so late?

Ivy frowned. "He left quite angry with me. He probably needs time to cool down."

Myrtle looked at Ivy. "Yes, he'll come back once he's has time to process it all."

"And the plan?" Margaret said.

Myrtle patted her white hair in place with her multi-ringed fingers. "That's a good question, Ivy. What's the plan?"

Ivy rose from her chair. "I've been thinking about that since yesterday." She handed a coffee cup to Margaret.

"And?" Margaret asked as she poured herself a cup.

"I know one thing for sure. We can't do this alone. We're going to need Salina's help."

"Salina? How will we find her?" Margaret asked.

Myrtle smirked. "Oh, we can find her."

Margaret's head spun. Maybe she'd slept too long. She stood at the end of the table.

As Ivy sat back down, she and Myrtle

exchanged some sort of silent communication.

"What?" Margaret snapped. "What are you two thinking?"

Ivy sighed. "Sit down, my dear." After Margaret sat, Ivy continued, "I told you at the mounds there was some bad karma at play here."

Margaret nodded, not really understanding what the point was.

"Karma must be broken. We might be able to get your daughter back, but if the cycle isn't severed, this will happen again to another child, and again after that. It's been a never-ending repetition of events for two thousand years."

Margaret propped her elbows on the table and rubbed her temples. "What does that have to do with Salina? How can she help?"

Myrtle lifted her cup to her red-lipstick-coated lips. "She's not going to help."

"You're wrong, Myrtle," Ivy said. "She has to help. She's the one who started this cycle and she's the only one who can end it. I'm sure she'll help. She helped us get away last time, didn't she?"

Myrtle frowned. "I still don't understand why she did that."

"I know exactly why she did it. She was feeling guilty for all those children for all those years. We're going to use that bit of information to end this once and for all."

"What kind of leverage can we use to convince her to help?" Myrtle asked.

Ivy grinned and tilted her head toward Margaret.

Myrtle looked questioningly at Ivy, then at Margaret, and her face brightened.

Ivy and Myrtle smiled at each other and both turned to Margaret.

"What?" Margaret asked. "What are you looking at?"

"Yes, I think it'll work," Myrtle winked at Ivy.

Ivy nodded.

Margaret squinted at the old women. "If either of you would care to tell me what the plan is, I'd be happy to listen."

Myrtle placed her cup on the table. "We'll get to that in a minute." She looked at Ivy, "And it is a brilliant plan. I do have one question, though. What if Oma decides to kill us this time?"

Ivy shrugged. "If she does, she does. We've lived long enough, don't you think?"

Myrtle smirked. "You know, over the years, I've had to wonder if it was just an idle threat. What if she can't kill us?"

"I've thought that myself, but there's no doubt in my mind she could destroy us both if she wanted to."

Margaret groaned. "I'm really having trouble understanding any of this."

Ivy patted Margaret's hand. "You'll understand it all by tonight, I promise."

Myrtle rose and clapped her hands. "Well, we'd better get moving if we're going to get Sarah back."

***

By 3:00 PM, the three women were on their way to the mounds in Ivy's old car, with Ivy at the wheel, Myrtle in the passenger seat, and Margaret in the back.

"How do you know we can get Sarah back?"

Margaret asked.

"Well, we've done it before," Myrtle said. "Once."

"Only once?"

Myrtle nodded. "I tried a couple times and failed, but the last time we tried to rescue a child, we succeeded."

"I'd ask you what happened when you failed, but I don't want to know."

"No, you don't want to focus on that, dear."

Margaret felt tension floating through the car like water rising. She was having trouble catching her breath. She closed her eyes. Breathe in. Breathe out. Slowly. In. Out. Finally, she said, "What I really want to know is how you succeeded." She opened her eyes. Ivy was gripping the steering wheel so tightly; her knuckles were white.

"That was the time Salina helped," Ivy said.

"Yes, Salina stood up to Oma and convinced her to let us go," Myrtle added.

"Will this Oma make an appearance?"

"Yes," the elderly women said simultaneously, sending a shiver down Margaret's spine.

Margaret looked out the window and watched the trees go by. They must've been going a whole twenty miles per hour. She wished Ivy would drive faster. Margaret wanted to hurry, but she had to admit she was terrified to get there. The only sound in the car was the humming of the engine.

"How do we find them?" Margaret asked.

"We don't have to find them. They'll find us," Ivy said. "I told you before I hadn't been to the mounds in a long time, right?"

"Yes."

"Well, the reason I haven't been there—actually neither of us has been there—is we've been hiding out from Oma for thirty-nine years. The moment we arrive at the mounds, she'll know."

"But we were there the other day."

"Yes, and she knew it then, and she'll know when we return," Ivy said.

"Will they just show up when we get there?" Margaret asked.

Myrtle spoke up. "Oh, they'll be there. Don't worry about that. We are most assuredly going to have a battle on our hands with Oma tonight, but Salina will help make it right. She is the one who began the evil, and she will help us end it."

"How again are you going to convince her to help?"

Ivy and Myrtle glanced at each other.

"It shouldn't be too much of a problem," Ivy said.

"And what about Oma?" Margaret asked.

"Yeah, that's a problem," Myrtle said.

Lori Crane

Chapter 26

The Call

As the women pulled into the parking lot at Bynum Mounds, they found the place empty. The police tape had been removed from the entrance, and there was no police cruiser standing guard. No volunteers, no ladies handing out donuts and coffee, no search teams or canine units.

Margaret slumped in the seat. "They've forgotten Sarah already."

"We haven't," Ivy assured her.

The parking spaces ran parallel with the field. Ivy pulled into the farthest corner of the lot and parked facing the field, the car crossing three parking spaces. She turned off the engine, and it sputtered before going silent. They stared at the field before them.

Margaret asked, "So, what do we do now?"

"We wait," Ivy said. "She knows we're here." She turned around to look at Margaret. "Margaret, I'm going to be blunt with you."

"Okay," Margaret said uncomfortably.

"The Maggie I remember was a brave and headstrong young girl. She had a mind of her own and she was not afraid of anything. I'm not sure what has happened to you over the years, but you seem to have lost your way. The truth of the situation is, if you want to save your daughter, you need to bring back that brave girl today. The Maggie I remember wouldn't back down from a challenge. Most times, she ran headfirst into encounters. The bigger, the better. We need that Maggie back today in full force."

"I'm not sure that Maggie exists anymore."

"If you want your daughter back, you need to dig down into the depths of your being and find her, and you need to bring her to the forefront right now. This is not going to be an easy task. As a matter of fact, this is going to be impossible, but we're going to do it anyway."

Myrtle didn't take her eyes off the overgrown field.

"I don't know how to be strong anymore," Margaret said, wishing she could explain how hard her life was, how rocky her marriage was, but knowing this wasn't the time to wallow in self-pity.

"Strength is a choice, Margaret. You can be brave or you can lose your daughter. Those are the only two options available to you right now," Myrtle said. After a moment, she added, "The worst that will happen here today is our own demise. If you're not afraid to die for your daughter, we have a chance to be victorious. But if you doubt yourself, Oma will know. She will use it against you. You need to be crystal clear in your own mind of what's important. Your daughter is important. Nothing else is. The only thing stopping you from saving Sarah is your own fear. You can allow it to immobilize you or you can force it down and move forward and do what needs to be done."

Margaret thought about her past, her present, her future. She thought of her childhood, her mother, her college days, her marriage. She thought of her husband, her children. No, she wasn't afraid to die. She was afraid she'd lose her daughter forever. She was afraid of being a failure as a mother. She was afraid of not being loved by her husband. She was afraid of many, many things, but at this moment, death wasn't one of them.

She sat up a little taller and scanned the tree line on the other side of the field. Why did she suddenly have the impression they were being watched? Though she didn't see anyone, she knew someone was there. A small fire grew in her gut. Yes, she would be strong. She would face this demon she wasn't even sure she believed in. For Sarah, she would fight these witches until her very last breath if she must. "They're here," she said quietly.

The ladies waited.

Margaret's cell phone rang in her purse, filling the car with a computerized song of gawdy happiness. At any other time, the sound would have startled her. Not now. At this moment, she felt surprisingly calm. She couldn't remember the last time she'd felt this sure of what she was doing and why. She dug the phone out and looked at the screen. It was the sheriff's number.

"Hello?"

"Hi, Mrs. Speedwell. This is Sheriff Miller."

"Hello, Sheriff. Any news?"

"No, ma'am, I'm afraid not. I just wanted to bring you up to date. We've suspended the physical search for your daughter. The deputies will continue to actively pursue any and all leads, but we have sent the volunteers home."

"I'm at the Bynum Mounds and it's empty, so I guess I already realized that."

"Well, ma'am, if you have any questions, you can always call me back at this number."

"Okay, Sheriff, thank you for calling."

She disconnected the call.

Ivy looked at Margaret in the rearview mirror. "Would you like some privacy to call your husband?"

Margaret, looked back at the phone in her hand and nodded.

The ladies stepped out of the car.

Margaret dialed her husband.

"Thomas?"

"Hi, Margaret. I was just about to call you. I'm on my way down."

"You are?"

"Yes. Sheriff Miller called about the search."

"I already know. He called me, too."

"Are you okay?"

She paused. "Yes, I'm okay."

He didn't respond.

"How's Emily?" she asked.

"She's still not speaking, but she seems to be okay otherwise. She's been going to school every day. Her teacher has been very supportive. My mother is still staying at the house and we found a psychologist to work with Emily. We have an appointment for an evaluation on Monday."

"That's good. I miss her."

"She misses you, too." After a moment, he added, "So do I."

Margaret didn't know how to respond.

"Are you still there?" he asked.

"Yes, yes, I'm here. Listen, I need to tell you what's been going on here, and I'm not sure where to start."

"I'll be there in an hour or so. Do you want to wait and talk in person?"

"Um, yeah, that might be best. It's a pretty crazy story."

"Okay, we'll talk when I get there. Are you sure you're okay with them calling off the search?"

"Yes, it's all right."

"Really? I would have thought the news would have sent you into a tailspin." He awaited a response but none came. "You sound different. Are you alone right now? It sounds quiet there."

"No, no tailspins, and no, I'm not alone. I'm with Rich's grandmother and her friend."

"Oh, that's nice. I bet they've been a good support system for you."

"Yes, you have no idea."

"That's good. Do you think you want to come home now that they've called off the search?"

She didn't answer.

"Margaret?"

"I'm sorry, I don't know the answer to that right now. There are other things at play here but yes, I'd like to come home."

"Okay, that's good. You sound a little strange. Are you sure you're all right?"

"I'm all right. I'll see you when you get here, okay?"

"Okay."

He sounded as if he was going to hang up, but he didn't.

"Thomas?"

"Hmm."

"Listen, if anything happens to me…"

"What do you mean?"

"Just listen. If anything happens to me, please tell Emily I love her."

"Now you're worrying me."

"Don't worry. I'll see you soon."

She disconnected before he had a chance to respond, and she climbed out of the car. She tossed her phone onto the backseat and closed the door.

Chapter 27

Confrontation

Ivy and Myrtle had waded through the calf-high grass and stopped in the center of the field. They stood facing the woods.

"Hey, wait up," Margaret called.

Myrtle turned and put her hand up for Margaret to stop where she was.

Margaret froze as she saw a woman emerging from the woods. The woman approached Myrtle and Ivy, cautious and wide-eyed like a frightened deer. She was young, with long black hair and a slender figure. Who was this? It couldn't possibly be Oma or Salina. The woman didn't seem to notice Margaret. The body language of the approaching woman was tense, but Ivy and Myrtle seemed at ease. They obviously knew the woman. The trio spoke for at least ten minutes while Margaret remained still.

Finally, they turned and headed toward Margaret. A shiver of apprehension went up her spine. When they were about one hundred yards away, the stranger froze, staring at Margaret as if terrified.

Ivy called to Margaret. "Stay right there. I'd like you to meet Salina." She turned to Salina and laughed. "Salina, you look like you've seen a ghost. Come and say hello."

Salina resumed walking, cautiously, one small step at a time. The trio reached Margaret.

Ivy made the introduction. "Salina, this is our dear friend, M—"

"Mia?" Salina said.

Myrtle laughed. "That's the first thing I thought, too."

"No, Salina," Ivy said. "This is not Mia. This is Margaret."

Myrtle added, "From what I remember, she does bear a striking resemblance to Mia. Of course, that was a very long time ago."

Salina's dark skin had turned pale, and she looked as if she may run away at any moment.

"The least you can do is say hello, Salina," Ivy said.

Salina didn't say anything, her eyes on Margaret's face. The corners of her mouth turned down and her bottom lip trembled.

"It's nice to meet you," Margaret mumbled, looking to Ivy and Myrtle for guidance. Is this one of the witches everyone was so afraid of? She looked like a sixteen-year-old girl. And right now, she looked more frightened than anything.

"Salina is deciding whether she can help us," Ivy said.

"What would help her make her decision?" Margaret turned to Salina. "What can we do?"

Salina shook her head, still staring at Margaret. Tears filled her eyes.

Ivy continued as if she didn't notice. "Salina knows where Sarah is. Don't you, Salina?"

Salina nodded. A tear ran down her cheek.

"You know where my daughter is?" Margaret asked.

Salina nodded again.

"Are you the one who took her?"

Another tear fell. "Yes," Salina said.

Margaret felt her face redden with anger. "Why?"

"I'm sorry, so very sorry. I didn't have a choice."

"One always has a choice."

"Oma will kill me if I don't do as she demands. There is no choice. It is the price I had to pay. I had to take the baby."

Margaret's brow furrowed. "Sarah's no baby."

Myrtle stepped in. "She's getting you confused with Mia."

Salina looked at Myrtle. "This isn't Mia?"

"No. This is Margaret."

"But she looks just like M...M..."

"Yes, we know," Myrtle said.

"So, Margaret," Ivy said, "Salina thinks we can get Sarah back. She doesn't know how we will defend ourselves against Oma, but I guess the three of us will have to deal with Oma once we get you and Sarah to safety."

Margaret shook her head. "No, no, I will not leave you to fight this battle alone. Tell me what you need me to do."

Ivy smiled. "Now that's the brave, young girl I know and love." She looked at the other ladies. "Let's figure out a plan to pull Oma out into the open."

The women spent the next couple of hours deciding how to best approach Oma, how to get Sarah back safely, and how to keep from getting killed in the process. As the sun softened behind the trees, they put their plan into action.

Chapter 28

Ticking Clock

Thomas banged on the screen door. "Rich? Rich Martin, are you here?"

Rich appeared and opened the screen door. "Mr. Speedwell. What are you doing here?"

"Is Margaret here?"

"No, she's not. I guess she's out with my grand…with Ivy and Myrtle."

"Do you know what's going on with her? She called me and didn't sound right."

"What do you mean?" He backed out of the doorway. "I'm sorry, come in. Can I get you a drink?"

Thomas entered. In the living room were piles of clothes on the sofa and the big easy chair. Suitcases were strewn about the floor. "Are you going somewhere?"

"Yes, excuse the mess. I'm packing."

"Oh." Thomas wanted to ask where Rich was going, but he was more concerned about his wife. "Do you know what's happening with Margaret?"

"I…um…sort of."

"Then please explain it to me. She didn't sound like herself on the phone. And to top it all off, the sheriff called off the search for Sarah, so now I'm very worried about Margaret's mental state. I don't think she's strong enough to handle news like this."

Rich rubbed the back of his neck. "I'm really

sorry to hear that about Sarah. If you want to know the whole story, you'd better come and sit down and let me pour you a drink." He walked down the hall toward the kitchen, expecting Thomas to follow.

After Rich gave Thomas the abbreviated version, Thomas sat stunned at the kitchen table, trying to absorb some crazy story about witches and missing children. "Is this the nonsense you've been filling my wife's head with? Witches riding around on brooms, snatching kids from their parents? What are they going to do with them? Fatten them up to put in a stew? No wonder Margaret sounded so strange on the phone."

"I assure you it's not nonsense. I know it's hard to believe, but it's all true."

"I can't even wrap my head around what kind of craziness is going on here," Thomas said as he rose to his feet. "I'm going to go find my wife."

By the time he put his key into the ignition, Rich had jumped into the passenger seat, uninvited. "I can't let you go alone. If all of this is like the old women say it is, you need more friends, not fewer. Let's look first at the mounds. Maybe they went there."

The two sped toward the Bynum Mounds.

Chapter 29

The Battle

Salina jammed the torch into the ground in the center of the field. Its golden light glittered across the tall grasses. Spinning slowly, Salina called out, "Oma."

Myrtle, Ivy, and Margaret remained hidden in the bushes.

Salina called for Oma again.

Something rustled in the tree line. An owl hooted in the distance, announcing nightfall. The full moon was rising, but its blue light was no match for the glow of the torch. After another rustle, a figure emerged from the forest. The hairs on Margaret's arms stood straight up.

The hooded figure approached Salina, seemingly floating across the land, the long black cloak dragging behind on the ground. Margaret could not see the figure's face, as it was shrouded by a large hood, but she imagined the ugliest old witch possible.

"Where are they?" the figure asked.

"They're here," Salina replied.

"Did you restrain them as I asked?"

"No, Oma, I didn't. But they are here, and they wish to speak with you."

"Why would I want to speak with them? I have nothing to say to those traitors." She raised her arm and a bolt of lightning snapped a tree in half right behind her. It crashed to the ground, the seared end glowing, smoke from the charred bark rising into the air.

Margaret gasped. *This is the power this witch has? We are all dead*, she thought.

"Oma, please listen to them. This has gone on long enough."

"Are you rebelling? What have I told you about that?" Oma raised her hand and a rope of vines emerged from the tree line, snaking across the ground toward Salina. Even if Salina turned and ran, she would be no match for their speed. They crawled up Salina's legs, her torso, her arms, binding her tightly. "I've told you over and over what would happen to you if you crossed me. You are nothing, a little flea under my shoe."

Ivy stepped out. "That's enough, Oma. Let her go!"

"Ah, there you are," Oma cackled. "I knew that would make you come out of your little hiding spot." She pushed the hood off, revealing a young and beautiful woman, her black hair shining in the light of the torch.

Margaret was stunned. This was not an ugly witch that children learn of in storybooks. This was a beautiful creature.

"Oma, you are finished kidnapping children," Ivy said as she boldly approached Oma.

"You are in no position to tell me what to do. I spared you the last time, but you will not be so fortunate this time."

Myrtle stepped out onto the field. "We are not your children anymore."

"You are anything I say you are." Oma grabbed a ball of fire from the torch and hurled it at Myrtle.

Myrtle waved it off with a flick of her wrist. It vaporized, the ashes dropping at her feet. It all happened so fast, Margaret wasn't sure she'd seen it correctly.

"A little out of practice?" Oma taunted, attempting to disavow Myrtle's quick reflexes.

"We want the girl you've taken," said Ivy, stopping about fifty yards from Oma.

Oma rose higher into the air. "You cannot have her." She laughed and spun.

"You will give her to us or we will take her," Myrtle said.

Oma's cloak was swirling around her. "You don't even know where she is, but I'll tell you what. We'll have a little wager. If you can defeat me, you can have her."

Ivy waved both arms, and a glowing blue wall appeared between her and Oma.

"You think that will work?" Oma laughed again, this time sounding like a hyena from the gates of hell. "Your parlor tricks don't impress me." Oma threw a dozen fireballs toward Ivy and Myrtle.

They bounced off the blue barrier, emitting a sizzle with each strike. The color of the barrier changed with each fireball that connected, as if the barrier was faltering.

Myrtle said, "Not only do we want the child back, but we will never let you kidnap another child. You are finished destroying lives."

"Do you think I destroyed your life? Look at you. I made you immortal. Both of you. I call that giving you life, not destroying it. You'd be long dead if it weren't for me."

Ivy formed a glowing green ball of light between her hands. "If you made us immortal, why do you think you can kill us? If it's true that you can kill us, that means we can kill you, too."

Oma stopped spinning and formed her own ball, a radiant red orb. "Are you threatening to destroy me? What kind of threat is that?"

"It's the only kind you understand." Ivy tossed her ball of light at Salina. Salina's bonds sizzled and vanished. Salina ran into the woods. Oma ignored her.

Oma hurled her ball of fire at Ivy. It crackled through what was left of the blue barrier. Ivy was too slow to stop it. It hit her head-on and she collapsed on the ground without a sound. The barrier vanished.

Without thinking, Margaret ran from her hiding place to help Ivy.

"Oh, who's this?" Oma said.

"You leave her alone," shouted Myrtle.

Oma chuckled. "I can't believe you brought a mortal along with you to challenge me." She formed another red fireball and threw it at Margaret.

Myrtle leapt in front of the ball and took the full force of the blow. She collapsed on the grass next to Ivy.

Margaret knelt on the ground next to Ivy, who wasn't moving. She couldn't tell if Ivy was still breathing. "Grandma Ivy, are you okay? Wake up."

Nothing.

"Grandma, please."

Nothing.

She glanced over at Myrtle, who looked the same. She was now alone in fighting this being. She rose to her feet and faced Oma. "How could you do this? They're dead! You've killed them! Is this what you do to your children? That's what you called them, right? Your children?"

"You know nothing of this, girl. Why don't you

run along now before you get hurt?"

Margaret looked around for a weapon. She saw nothing to use, only a sea of overgrown grass.

Tires squealed from the parking lot behind her and she turned to see Thomas and Rich jumping out from the Mercedes, the headlights shining across the field. Thank God they were here.

But they froze at the sight before them.

"Do you think they're going to help you? You're mistaken. If they do, I'll kill them also," Oma taunted.

Margaret yelled, "Thomas, don't move! Rich, stay there!"

She looked down at Ivy and Myrtle.

"I'm afraid your little witch friends are not powerful enough to help you, either. Poor little girl. What will you do?"

Margaret was wondering the same thing. She would have to fight this witch with her bare hands—no swords, no magic, no fireballs, only prayer and determination. She wasn't a strong person. She wasn't brave. She was quite certain she would die. The situation couldn't get any worse.

But it did.

As Margaret attempted to assess a weakness in Oma, Salina emerged from the woods, dragging Sarah by the arm. The sight of her daughter took Margaret's breath away for a moment. Thank God she was alive! But how could she save her daughter without Ivy and Myrtle's help? This wasn't the plan. Why did they not have a back-up plan? Why did they not formulate a plan B? She waited for Salina to give her some kind of sign. Nothing came. She glanced at her husband. He wasn't moving. She looked down at Ivy. Nothing. Margaret was so frightened, she was frozen, too. She looked back at Sarah and heard Ivy's voice in her head: *"If you want to save your daughter, you need to bring back that brave girl today."*

Time stood still.

Margaret saw a tear roll down Sarah's cheek.

She heard Myrtle's voice in her head this time: *"Strength is a choice, Margaret. You can be brave or you can lose your daughter."*

She took a deep breath and stood up straight. A fire was growing in her gut. Now if she could just find the courage to match.

"Momma!" Sarah cried.

Nothing could have brought out the lioness in Margaret more than those words and that voice. Margaret bolted toward Oma. As she passed the torch standing between them, she yanked it out of the ground with the strength of a warrior.

Oma formed another ball of fire and pulled her arm back to throw it, but before she could, Margaret lunged with the torch and pushed it into Oma's stomach, impaling her with fire.

Cobalt lightning bolts flew from Oma's center in every direction, filling the air with electricity. Sparks flew past Margaret, just missing her on all sides. Oma screamed, a simultaneous shriek and low moan. Margaret twisted the torch. More lightning flew. "This is for Mia!" She twisted again, shouting over Oma's screams. "This is for Rich!" She twisted harder. "This is for Myrtle!" Another twist. "And for Ivy!" And another. "This is for Sarah!" Each twist exuded more rage, more sadness, more fear, more determination, and more sparks. "This is for every child you've stolen!" Twist. "For every mother you've ever destroyed!" Twist. "For every ounce of evil you've brought into this world!" Twist. "Every malicious act that ruined families and children and lives!" Twist. "You deserve to burn in hell!"

Oma's screams grew louder, and toward the end, Margaret was also screaming at the top of her lungs. After the last twist of the torch, Oma collapsed, nothing left but a pile of smoldering ashes in the charred remains of a black cloak. The blue lightning sizzled and quickly vanished.

All was still.

Margaret looked up and saw Salina quietly sobbing. Salina let go of Sarah, who ran toward her mother.

"Momma?"

Margaret dropped the torch and fell to her knees and held her arms wide. Sarah ran to them. Margaret scooped the girl into her arms and held her tightly. She rocked back and forth on her knees, caressing the top of Sarah's head, kissing her over and over. "Are you okay?" she cried as she hugged Sarah. "Oh, baby, I'm so glad you're okay."

Chapter 30

Reconciliation

Thomas ran to his wife and daughter and wrapped his arms around them. The trio sat on the ground, hugging and crying.

Rich ran to Ivy and knelt down beside her. He grabbed her wrist, searching for a pulse. "Grandma?"

Myrtle came to and mumbled, "What happened?" She saw Margaret and Thomas across the field, holding Sarah. "Is it over?"

Rich said, "Yes, it's over." He shook Ivy's shoulders. "Grandma?"

Myrtle climbed to her knees and crawled toward Ivy. "Is she okay?"

Ivy didn't open her eyes but murmured, "I'm okay."

Rich laughed and kissed her hand. "I'm so glad you're all right."

Ivy opened her eyes and smiled. "I'm glad you're glad."

Tears of relief fell from his eyes, spotting Ivy's cotton dress.

Ivy sighed. "Rich, I'm so very sorry about everything. Please know I've always loved you and I raised you as very best I could."

"I know that. I guess no matter if we're blood or not, you'll always be my grandma."

"Yes, I will."

He helped her sit up and they hugged for a long time.

"We should go back to the house and give them some time alone," Ivy said, indicating Margaret and her family.

Rich nodded, helping her to her feet. "I'll drive."

As they walked to the car, Ivy looked at Myrtle. "Your lipstick is smeared," she said.

Myrtle laughed.

He got the women settled in Ivy's car. "I'll be right back."

He walked over to Margaret. "Are you all okay?"

Margaret nodded.

"See you back at the house?"

Margaret didn't respond. She was too wrapped up in her daughter.

Margaret heard Rich say something, but she didn't know what it was. For now, she could do nothing except hug her daughter. "Are you okay, honey? Momma missed you so very much."

"Daddy missed you, too," Thomas added.

"Where's Emily?" Sarah asked.

"She's at home with Grandma," Thomas answered.

"How did she get there? She was just here with us."

"Oh, honey," Margaret said. "Do you remember anything about what happened?"

Sarah wrinkled her face in thought. She shook her head, her blonde curls bouncing. She threw her arms around her mother's neck. "I love you, Momma."

"I love you, too, baby."

Margaret looked toward the woods. Salina was gone. Margaret looked for Ivy and Myrtle and saw them watching her from Ivy's car as Rich drove it out of the parking lot. Thank goodness they were okay.

"Let's get you home," Margaret said, and kissed Sarah on the forehead.

Thomas helped Margaret and Sarah across the field, and when they reached the Mercedes, he buckled Sarah into the backseat and closed the door.

As Margaret opened the passenger door, Thomas grabbed her arm.

"I don't claim to understand anything I saw out there. Rich told me some crazy story about witches, and I still don't believe it, even after what I just witnessed. But I have to tell you, I've never seen anyone act as bravely as you did. I'm absolutely amazed by what you did. If that were me out there, I'm afraid we wouldn't have our Sarah back."

She smiled at him. It had been a long time since he looked into her eyes with this much love. Maybe their marriage was now on the right track again. "We have our Sarah back, and as soon as you can get us home, we'll be a family again."

He kissed her deeply. "I love you, Margaret Speedwell."

"Call me Maggie, okay?"

He grinned. "Okay, you got it."

They kissed again.

"Take us home," Margaret whispered into her husband's ear.

Sarah hollered from the backseat, "Let's go, you guys! That's gross!"

Margaret and Thomas laughed.

Chapter 31

Goodbyes

Rich was loading his suitcases into the trunk of his car when Margaret and her family arrived.

"Uh-oh, that doesn't look good," Margaret said.

"He said he was going somewhere, but I didn't ask for any details," Thomas said.

"Hmm. Okay, I'm going to go in and say goodbye."

Rich had gone back into the house.

"Do you need me to help you get your things?"

"No, I just have the one bag. You stay here with Sarah. I'll be back in a moment."

Margaret went inside but didn't see Rich. She heard voices in the kitchen so she headed down the hall.

"Oh, Margaret, I'm glad you came back. How's your little girl?" Ivy asked.

"She's fine. Doesn't remember anything. How are you?"

"Oh, we're both fine." Ivy nodded at Myrtle, who was sitting at the table drinking a large glass of sweet tea. "I was just putting some supper on the stove. Do you all want something to eat?"

"No, we're going to head home. I just wanted to come in and say goodbye and thank you for everything."

Ivy opened her arms for a hug. "You are more than welcome, my dear, and I'm glad everything ended well for your family."

Margaret heard the screen door slam. "I wish everything here could end well, also. Is he leaving?"

"I'm afraid he is, but when he thought I was dead out there in the field, he softened a bit. I think he'll come to terms with it eventually."

"Do you know where he's going?"

Ivy shook her head. "He didn't say."

"I'm really sorry." Margaret hugged her again.

"It's okay. He has every right to be angry." She changed the subject. "You need to bring your girls down for a visit. Will you do that? They can play in the pond and sleep in the room with the twin beds."

"They would love that! Yes, we'll come back very soon, I promise. Even though we aren't family, I feel like you're about the closest thing I have to family."

"We are family, dear. Family doesn't need to be blood. I'll always be your Grandma Ivy."

Margaret kissed her on the cheek. "Thank you again." She turned to Myrtle. "And thank you, Myrtle. You put yourself in danger to keep me safe. I don't know what I would have done without you both. I really mean it."

Myrtle smiled at her. "I'm glad you got your little girl back."

"Me, too! Well, I really must run. Thomas and Sarah are waiting in the car. I'm going to grab my things and I'll see you both again very soon."

She went to her room and crammed her toiletries and clothes into her bag. As she exited, she stopped in the doorway and looked around one last time. She would bring the girls here for a visit. Maybe not right away, but eventually. Her children would come to know and love Grandma Ivy. And Margaret would find a copy of that picture of the children and the angel for her daughters' room at home. It was important to know that everything in the world wouldn't always be right, but someone would be there to watch over you. She clicked off the light.

She walked out the screen door and held it so it wouldn't slam. She bounced down the steps and saw Rich leaning against his car, waiting for her.

"Is your little girl all right?"

Margaret nodded.

"Are y'all going home now?"

She nodded again. "What about you?"

"What about me?"

"Where are you going with all your suitcases packed?"

"Oh, I don't know. I guess I'll start with a trip down to the Gulf to clear my head for a while." He paused. "Then I was thinking I'd go to Memphis."

"That sounds like a great idea."

He hugged her and kissed her on the cheek. "Bye, Maggie."

"Bye, Rich."

She backed away, watching him for a few steps. Then she turned and walked to the Mercedes.

Thomas backed out of the driveway as Margaret watched Rich climb into his old Lincoln. Thomas blinked the headlights and waved as he turned onto the road. They headed north.

Rich followed them out of the driveway and headed south.

Ivy and Myrtle stood on the front porch, watching the taillights disappear in both directions.

Lori Crane

Chapter 32

Home

After the car engines could no longer be heard, Ivy turned toward the door. "I guess we should go in and have some supper. It's late."

A voice called from the darkness near the end of the driveway. "Can I come up?"

Ivy turned back. "Yes, Salina, you're welcome to come up."

Salina walked slowly, her moccasins silent on the gravel drive. The dim porchlight barely lit her face, but her black hair glistened as if made of satin. As she neared the porch, she said, "I really don't have any place to go."

Ivy looked at Myrtle and Myrtle nodded.

"You are welcome to stay here, Salina," Ivy said.

"Really? That's very kind of you." She stopped at the bottom of the steps. "I owe you both an apology. I'm sorry for everything you went through because of me."

Myrtle stepped forward. "It wasn't because of you. It was because of Oma. Don't beat yourself up."

"I want you both to know how deeply sorry I am."

Myrtle reached out her hand. Salina took it and climbed the steps. Myrtle escorted her toward the door. "Well, you can't be mad at family forever, and you are my aunt Salina."

"Yes, I am. I was thinking I don't have anyone now, but I guess I still have you."

"Of course, you do. Let's go inside and have some supper," Ivy said.

Myrtle and Salina walked arm in arm into the house. Ivy looked out one last time in the direction Rich had driven. Then she entered the house, letting the screen door slam behind her.

As the three talked in the kitchen, a small seed popped open in the front yard, and the tiniest blade of grass took root under the pecan trees.

The End

About the Author

Lori Crane is a native Mississippi belle currently residing in greater Nashville, Tennessee. She is a professional musician by night, an indie author by day.

Her literary awards and achievements include:

- Bronze medal in literary fiction at the 2013 eLit Book Awards for *Okatibbee Creek*.
- Honorable mention in historical fiction at the 2013 Midwest Book Festival for *Okatibbee Creek*.
- Finalist in the 2014 Eric Hoffer Awards for *An Orphan's Heart*.
- Honorable mention in general fiction at the 2013 Midwest Book Festival for *Elly Hays*.
- Shortlisted for 50 Self-published Books Worth Reading in 2013/14 at Indie Author Land for *Elly Hays*.
- *Elly Hays* debuting at #1 on Amazon Kindle in Native American stories.

- *The Legend of Stuckey's Bridge* featured on the 2018 season of *Most Terrifying Places in America* on the Travel Channel.
- Listed in the top 23 bestselling historical fiction authors on Amazon.

Lori is a member of the United Daughters of the Confederacy, Daughters of the American Revolution, United States Daughters of 1812, and the Screen Actors Guild-American Federation of Television and Radio Artists. For more info, visit LoriCrane.com.

Other Books by Lori Crane

The Okatibbee Creek Series
Okatibbee Creek
An Orphan's Heart
Elly Hays

The Stuckey's Bridge Trilogy
The Legend of Stuckey's Bridge
Stuckey's Legacy: The Legend Continues
Stuckey's Gold: The Curse of Lake Juzan

The Culpepper Saga
I, John Culpepper
John Culpepper the Merchant
John Culpepper, Esquire
Culpepper's Rebellion

Other Titles
Savannah's Bluebird
Witch Dance
On This Day: A Perpetual Calendar for Family Genealogy
The Culpepper-Fairfax Scandal
Eula

Lori Crane

An Excerpt from

The Legend of Stuckey's Bridge

Lori Crane

1942, Lauderdale County, Mississippi

Billy yanked up on his fishing pole. His eight-year-old brother asked, "Did you catch somethin'?"

Billy frowned as he watched the tip of his pole arc. The line grew taut. "Naw, I think I'm just snagged," he grumbled.

"Oh, I though you got a catfish."

"I wish. I think I'm stuck on somethin'." He lifted his pole again, reeling in an inch or two of the line.

"Maybe you caught one of Old Man Stuckey's boots."

"Don't even say that, Bobby. It gives me the creeps."

The warm afternoon sun quickly disappeared behind ominous dark clouds, leaving the boys in an eerie dusk one usually witnesses just before nightfall.

Bobby looked up. "It's gonna rain. You better get that line in so we can go."

Billy looked up, too. A gust of wind caught the front wisp of his brown hair and gave him a chill.

"You know, everyone says he's still here," Bobby snickered.

"Who?"

"Old Man Stuckey."

"Yeah, I know, but I'd rather not think about it. Besides, I'm a little busy at the moment." Billy wrinkled his forehead as he tugged on the line again, ever so slowly bringing it closer.

Bobby yelled into the air. "Old Man Stuckey, jump in there and unsnag that line." He giggled.

Billy didn't think it was funny and gave his younger brother a nasty look. "Don't call him," he whispered as if someone might hear him, even though he knew there wasn't a soul within miles of them.

Bobby rose from his seat on the bank, leaving his line dangling in the murky water. "Here, let me help you." He walked in front of Billy and reached out over the river, trying to grab the clear fishing line.

Billy lifted the pole into the air a third time, bending the tip. "Whatever it is, it's coming. It's just slow."

"Maybe it's the noose they hung him with." Bobby laughed.

Billy didn't.

The sunny afternoon was transforming into an oncoming storm, and the clouds were rolling in fast—gloomy, thick, menacing clouds. The breeze rustled Billy's hair again, making him shiver.

To the right of the young boys stood Stuckey's Bridge—a ninety-year-old bridge, one hundred twelve feet long, with a plank bottom and iron framework across the top. Some people fished from the top of the bridge, but Billy refused to step onto it. Bobby teased him incessantly about his fear of Old Man Stuckey's ghost, but Billy accepted the teasing and stayed firmly on the bank. The only reason he came out here at all was to catch the *big* catfish, and *they* lived under the bridge. As far as he knew, across the river stood nothing but trees and brush and the occasional woodland animal. In his twelve years of life, he never dared go across the bridge to see if there was more.

Bobby grabbed the line and took a step back,

pulling it as he moved. "What the heck you got on here?"

When Bobby let go, Billy spun the reel, bringing in the line a foot or so. "I don't know, probably just a branch or some leaves from the bottom."

"Well, whatever it is, it's heavy." Bobby stepped forward to get another handful of the line.

A crow flew overhead, barely maintaining its airborne status in the strong gusts of wind. Billy looked up for a moment, thinking the crow to be a bad omen. His hands began to sweat on the cork handle of his fishing pole. He decided at that very moment it was time to go, and they both needed to bring their lines in quickly. "Bobby, I got it from here. You should pull in your line so we can get home. Looks like a big storm comin'."

Bobby looked up at the sky. "Yeah, okay." He let go of Billy's line and walked back over to his fishing spot. A quick movement on the other side of the river caught his eye. "What was that?"

"What was what?" said Billy, still concentrating on his line.

"Over there." Bobby pointed to the left across the river. "I saw somethin' in the trees."

Billy looked over but didn't see anything. "Probably a possum or somethin'." Then Billy heard something in the brush. He froze.

Bobby heard it, too. "I told you I saw somethin'. Maybe a bobcat?"

Thunder cracked like a cannon above the boys' heads and made them jump. Bobby grabbed his pole and frantically reeled his line in. It was quickly growing dark and the wind was increasingly stronger. He watched Billy pull and tug at the line.

"It's almost free," Billy assured him. "It's comin' faster."

Bobby looked at the other side of the river. "Dang! There it is again. There's somethin' over there all right."

Billy glanced across the river, but with the dimming light, he couldn't see anything even if it was there. He pulled his line harder. A twig snapped across the river. Both boys darted their gazes in that direction but saw nothing but darkening woods.

"Maybe it's him!" Bobby teased.

"Stop it! Don't be stupid, Bobby."

Billy slowly but deliberately reeled in the line. He pointed the tip of his pole toward the water to keep it from snapping with the weight of the mystery catch, and he kept turning the reel. A drop of rain fell on his forehead, mingled with the nervous sweat on his brow, and gave him another shiver.

"Hurry up, Billy. We're gonna get soaked."

"I am hurrying. I don't want to break my line."

The crow sounded loudly from across the river, and shot straight up above the tree line as fast as an arrow released from a bow. The boys looked that way, knowing something was in the woods, just out of sight. Another branch snapped.

"What the heck is that?" Bobby sounded nervous, staring into the encroaching darkness on the other side of the river.

Billy didn't answer. He was absorbed in the blob he was dragging across the top of the murky water.

Bobby looked out at the greenish-brown blob. "You got nothin' but leaves. Let's go."

Billy pulled the blob onto the edge of the bank

and laid his pole on the ground. He moved toward the blob to dislodge his hook, and noticed something shining in the blob. *What is that? It's shimmering. What the...?*

Another branch snapped across the river.

"Come on, Billy. We gotta go. Now."

"Hold on," Billy said as he grabbed a stick and poked into the blob, separating the leaves and muck.

Yes, there was something shiny. *Something gold.*

Thunder rumbled. A rustling sound came from across the river, making Bobby look in that direction again. Heavy, fat raindrops splattered on their heads, and dead leaves began to whirl around the banks of the river in the increasing winds. *It's something round.* The crow cawed noisily. Another twig snapped. *It's a watch.* Thunder roared again. *On a gold chain.* Lightning lit the sky in a jagged pulse for a few short seconds. The wind intensified.

"What is that?" Bobby asked.

"It's a pocket watch." Billy reached down and rubbed the mud off the front of the watch. He cocked his head to the side and saw a single T embossed in the gold. Simultaneously, the thunder roared, the crow cawed, the rustle across the river grew louder, and to their right, a giant splash scared both boys into standing straight up.

They stared, mouths agape, in the direction of the bridge. Right under it, the water rippled in a circle as if something very, very large had just been dropped off the bridge. Thunder rumbled again. The water rippled more. The boys froze. An inch above the water in the center of the ripple was an eerie green glow. Instead of dissipating as they expanded, the ripples seemed to grow larger and higher in the ever-growing circle, as if the ocean tide was causing waves to come ashore.

The boys didn't look at each other. They didn't communicate. They turned at the same time and ran away as fast as their feet would carry them. They didn't grab their fishing poles. They didn't look back.

Lightning flashed while raindrops splattered the rocks, turning them from gray to brown. As the storm strengthened, the ripples inched up onto the bank, and little by little, pulled the gold pocket watch back into the murky depths.

25724468R00126

Made in the USA
Columbia, SC
07 September 2018